Banquet of Forgiveness Trilogy

Unavoided Struggles

by
E. M. Bennett

Unavoided Struggles

Trilogy Christian Publishers A Wholly Owned Subsidiary of Trinity Broadcasting Network

2442 Michelle Drive Tustin, CA 92780

Cover design by: Natalee Dunning

For information about special discounts for bulk purchases, please contact Trilogy Christian Publishing.

Manufactured in the United States of America

10 9 8 7 6 5 4 3 2 1

Library of Congress Cataloging-in-Publication Data is available.

ISBN: 978-1-68556-472-8

E-ISBN: 978-1-68556-473-5

*This book is dedicated to the Holy Spirit
who made this writing possible,
and to Melanie and Rick for allowing me
some solitude to work in their home.*

TABLE OF CONTENTS

———

CHAPTER ONE

Waking up to melodious sounds of multiple birds, Trent laid in his bed, taking it all in. He wondered if they were actually communicating with God or to each other. If with God, were they praising Him for another beautiful day? If to each other, were they simply greeting each other by saying good morning? He thought about their different distinct songs. Did each species recognize their native song just as humans recognize their native tongue? He realized humans can relate to each other simply through a smile, whether they understood the language each other spoke or not. A smile passed through all cultural barriers. Was it the same for birds or any other animal species?

Closing his eyes again, he laid in silent prayer, thanking the Lord that he woke up. He knew there were many in the world who wouldn't wake up this day. Another reason he had a yearning in his heart was to reach the less fortunate. If for some reason people wouldn't wake up to see another day on this side of eternity, he wanted to make sure they would wake up on the right side.

He smiled, knowing in just a few days, he would be traveling with his church's missions team to Ethiopia. He never thought, in all of his now nineteen years of life, that he would be traveling to Africa. To say he was excited would be an understatement. The moment God touched his heart and revealed Himself to Trent was the same moment He instilled a caring heart of love for unbelievers.

Trent knew at a very young age that everyone needed to know Jesus, or at least know about Him.

That is why he still struggled within himself concerning his biological father, Rus Arnold. Trent often tried to tell Rusty about Jesus, but he would shut the conversation down each time by telling Trent to quit talking about Him. Each time Trent vowed he'd never stop talking about Jesus. Trent had video-chat visits with Rusty ever since he moved from Arizona to Oregon. But Trent made sure he would email Rusty a Christian tract after each video visit with him. He told Rusty he would pray for him to receive Jesus and be saved. The court no longer had jurisdiction over Trent. He still chose to visit Rusty, but he spaced his visits few and far in between.

He found it quite discouraging to talk with Rusty. However, Trent knew in his heart that Jesus loved Rusty and died for him, just as He did all of humankind. All believers and all of the other discouraging unbelievers. Trent believed they just needed to hear the Word of God and the Truth so they could make an informative decision about Who Jesus is. Then hopefully, they would believe and be saved. Just looking at nature tells us there is a Creator and His name is God. There really is no excuse to be an unbeliever; they just don't know they have a choice. Trent realized people made excuses by having limited information. He knew, all in all, it is a choice. He just wanted Rusty, and as many unbelievers, he could reach to make the right choice.

In early March, nearly a month before Trent's nineteenth birthday on April 9th, Rev. Mauer began preparing his missions' team for the Ethiopian trip scheduled for the 31st of August. Trent tried sharing his exciting news with Rusty. Trent shared that he would be going to Ethiopia, but Rusty just snarled at the idea of Trent going to an African country.

"That makes no sense," Rusty said.

"The people there need to hear about Jesus. Therefore, it makes a lot of sense to me," Trent responded.

"Why should *those* people hear anything?" Rusty spat.

"*Those* people are no different than you. Many are unbelievers who need Jesus. The only difference between them and you is the fact that they will listen and hear the Good News and become saved," Trent had said in a firm voice.

"The only difference between *those* people and me is…" Rusty began, but Trent cut him off.

"Is that they are human beings that bleed like you, human beings that hurt like you and are human beings who need a Savior like you do," Trent said, interrupting Rusty's ignorant prejudice. He then stood up and closed his laptop, not to return.

Now six months later, Trent had three days to say goodbye to his family. He would call Rusty instead of seeing him on video. He didn't want the last couple of days before his trip to be tainted with Rusty's negativity. But first, he would go into the kitchen and have breakfast with his mom and dad.

"Good morning, Trent," Doug Milner said. Doug was the only father Trent knew. When his mother Abby finally married Doug years ago, none of the children took Doug's last name. They all stayed McLain's. But they all knew Doug as their dad. Nothing would ever change that.

"Good morning, Dad. Where's Mom?" he asked as he piled bacon and scrambled eggs onto his plate.

"She's getting ready for an early appointment with Dr. Rhonda," Doug explained.

"How's her sessions going? It's been about six years since the Albert incident," Trent asked.

The Albert incident. That's what they called the shooting of the intrusive drunk Albert Aguilar, who terrorized their family. They didn't talk about it aloud because they wanted to spare Trent's younger sister, Paisley, from the memory and unnecessary questions at her age. Paisley was now twelve years old, and she had questions for everything she heard. But Albert was not one of those things. She still didn't know or remember that Albert was her biological father.

"Her sessions are helping her a lot. She feels she's about finished with Dr. Rhonda, but new issues seem to arise. Now you're going out of the country, and that is an issue for her. But she'll get through this too," Doug answered.

"Good morning, Trent," Abby greeted her son.

"Good morning," he replied.

"I was talking to your grandma, and she wants to have us over for dinner tomorrow so we can all give you a proper send-off," she said as she sipped her coffee.

"I figured as much," Trent responded with a smile.

"Figured what?" a curious Paisley asked as she stepped into the kitchen and grabbed a plate to compile her breakfast on. Another reminder that she hears everything they openly talk about.

"Good morning, sweety. We were talking about having dinner at Grandma's place tomorrow to say goodbye to your brother," Abby quickly responded.

"That's right, you're leaving in a couple of days," Paisley said teasingly.

"You're going to miss me, little sister," Trent teased back.

"Miss, you hogging all of the bacon? No way!" she chided.

"We're all going to miss you, Trent," Abby let out a big sigh, then smiled at her son.

"Do you have everything packed yet?" Doug asked.

"Almost. I'm not sure how much to pack for a five-month trip," he said.

"Honey, I'll do the rest of your laundry tomorrow," Abby said, a little choked up, then excused herself to go to her appointment.

Trent watched his mom leave the room. He didn't know what to say, so he said nothing. He just continued eating his breakfast.

"Is Trista and the kids going to be there?" Paisley asked her dad.

"If I know your grandma, everyone will be there," Doug said, clearing his throat.

Trent asked to be excused then put his dishes in the sink. He went back to his room to sort through some family photos that he wanted to take. He had a wonderful photo of his mom and dad in a small picture frame. He put that into his suitcase. Then he decided to make the phone call that he dreaded.

Hearing the phone ring on the other end, Trent closed his eyes and whispered a quick prayer, "Lord, give me Your words." Then the person on the other end of the line answered.

"Hello?" came Rusty's voice.

"Hi Rusty, how are you doing?" Trent replied.

"My legs hurt, and I'm still alive," Rusty answered with his normal response.

"I'm leaving in a couple of days, and I just wanted to say goodbye," Trent stated.

"Right, you're going to Africa to tell the folks they need Jesus," Rusty responded.

"I am," was all that would come out of Trent's mouth.

"Don't come back with any diseases," Rusty said sarcastically.

Trent found himself flooded with little comments in his mind that he wanted to say to Rusty but knew not one of them would glorify the Lord. He was unable to speak for a moment.

"I'll call you when I get back home," Trent kindly said, then hung up the phone. Rusty was a challenge to converse with. Trent was grateful he wouldn't talk to old Rusty for several months.

Rusty heard the phone hang up on Trent's end. He felt a chill go down his spine as he realized he probably wouldn't talk to Trent again.

Abby pulled into the parking lot of Dr. Rhonda's office. She had arrived right on time. Abby didn't like to sit in the waiting room long. She found her mind would wander as she anticipated what issue Dr. Rhonda would want to address.

"Abby," Dr. Rhonda called out as she stood with the inner waiting room door wide open as if beckoning Abby to walk through it.

Abby rose to her feet and gave a cursory smile. Dr. Rhonda Finely, MS, who preferred to be called Dr. Rhonda, smiled back. Dr. Rhonda lead Abby down the long hallway to her office. Abby knew where it was but followed as if it were her first time. She noticed a new painting hung up in the hallway and smiled at the familiar artist's signature. J. McLain. Abby's mother.

"Nice painting," Abby blurted.

"Thank you for noticing," Dr. Rhonda said.

"How could I not? My mom has a style that I can recognize a mile away," she replied.

"Your mom?" Dr. Rhonda asked.

"That's one of my mother's paintings. Didn't you buy it from her?" Abby questioned.

Dr. Rhonda took a step back to look at the signature, then chuckled.

"I didn't realize it was your mother's work. My receptionist brought this in a couple of days ago. I forgot your maiden name is McLain," Dr. Rhonda explained.

"Just because you're the doctor who gets paid the big bucks, I guess I can't expect you to remember everything," Abby said a little sarcastically.

"I'm a psychologist, not an actual doctor of medicine, and furthermore, I'm human. I make mistakes," she said matter-of-factly.

"Right. I'm sorry, I'm not in a great mood," Abby tried to explain her sarcasm.

"Do you want to talk about it?" Dr. Rhonda asked.

"Well, in a nutshell, I'm experiencing another *significant emotional event*," Abby said, knowing now what that term meant. She had struggled with its meaning where her shooting Albert was concerned. But after a couple of years of exploring with Dr. Rhonda, she understood it.

"Okay. What is this new significant emotional event?" Dr. Rhonda asked.

"My son Trent is leaving for Ethiopia in three days," she sighed.

"For how long?" Dr. Rhonda probed.

"Five months."

"Okay, and that is putting you in a bad mood?" Dr. Rhonda asked.

"Not a bad mood, but a sad mood. My son has never been apart from me for that long," Abby admitted.

"I understand your sadness as a mother who is already missing her son, even though he's not gone yet," she began, "but should it cause you to be sad today?"

"Today, tomorrow, next month. What does it matter? My son is going to a dangerous country to share Jesus with unbelievers who may not want to hear about God's saving grace," she said with obvious tears in her eyes.

"So, you're worried?" Dr. Rhonda stated the question.

"I'm a mother. Of course, I'm worried. Or should I say, I'm concerned?" Abby asked, irritated at this questioning.

"I understand, Abby, but let me ask you, do you trust the Lord?"

"Yes," Abby replied, knowing where this was going.

"Then trust Him with your worry, fear, and concerns," Dr. Rhonda said.

"How do I do that?" she asked.

"Let God know your thoughts and ask the Lord to take them and give you peace knowing that He has Trent in His hands," she replied.

"Doesn't God already know my thoughts?" Abby asked.

"Yes, He does. But by you telling Him, it helps you to admit your concern out loud and enables you to hear yourself. Faith comes by hearing and hearing the Word of God, the Bible says, and in situations like this, you hear yourself contrary to God's Word. It's then you will hear God speak His truth again to you, so you do hear it. That's how He uses the Holy Spirit to talk to us. Deep down, we know the truth, but we question it sometimes. He reminds us of His truth, and then we hear ourselves speaking the truth out loud by answering our own questions with God's answers, thus increasing our faith in His truth, not our feelings. Do you understand what I'm saying?" Dr. Rhonda questioned.

"I think so. You mean I know the truth, but I choose to question what God says just so I can validate my feelings," Abby said.

"Abby, you have been listening over the past few years. I didn't even have to tell you that you're trying to justify your feelings. But please know your feelings are valid. Your son is going away from you physically. You will miss his presence. It's okay to grieve a temporary loss. But please keep in mind, it is temporary, and no matter what, God is with you and with Trent every second of every day," she added.

"I know. You're right, I just want others to be sad for me or with me. I should be happy and joyful that my son has a heart for unbelievers and is willing to go across the world to tell them about Jesus. What's wrong with me?" Abby questioned sincerely.

"Nothing."

"I want sympathy and a pity party instead of exercising my faith in God and trusting Him at His Word. I'm just so scared my son will get hurt," Abby confessed.

"You're a mother who loves her son. How do you think God felt when Jesus left His presence to go die for us?" Dr. Rhonda asked.

"I can't imagine," Abby admitted.

"Sure, you can. You're feeling a bit of it now, so you really can imagine. Maybe not entirely, but you can. This should make you feel closer to God. He really does understand you more than anyone else can," Dr. Rhonda closed their session on that note.

Abby left, feeling her head raised higher. For the first time since she gave her life to God, she felt a special bond with Him. She looked up confidently, smiling toward heaven before she got into her car. Once in, she started her car and said out loud, "Father, forgive my worry and fear. I know that You understand me. Help me through this and keep Trent safe from harm. Thank You."

CHAPTER TWO

It was late afternoon when Jandra McLain set the table for Trent's send-off dinner. One of his favorite meals was Mexican food, so Jandra prepared chicken enchiladas with rice and beans, while Mary Andrews, Jandra's mother, prepared a salad and made a French apple pie for dessert. The kitchen door opened, and Neil Sheppard, Jandra's best friend, walked in carrying two bags of tortilla chips.

"Here's your bags of tortilla chips," he said, handing them to Jandra and kissing Mary on the cheek as he walked past her.

"Thank you, Neil. I made salsa then realized I didn't have chips. Tortilla chips and salsa are the introduction to the dinner," Jandra rambled. Neil could sense she was a bit preoccupied in thought, as Jandra usually rambled on when she couldn't control a situation.

Rubbing her shoulders, he said, "It's okay. Just try to relax."

Jandra didn't like being told to relax, but she knew that's all she had to do. Trust God and take a deep breath. Everything would be all right.

The kitchen door flung open again, this time with Jandra's granddaughter Trista and her twin girls Sarah and Hanna, now four years old. Trista set a two-liter bottle of Pepsi down on the table while each girl struggled to lift the two-liter bottle they each carried onto the table. Neil quickly grabbed the bottles from the girls and set them down for them.

"Thank you," both girls said politely in unison.

"You're both very welcome and so polite," Neil said as he smiled and winked at Trista.

"Where's Jared and Ethan?" Mary asked, looking for Trista's husband and her first great-great-grandchild.

"They're coming. Jared was locking up when we left," Trista explained.

Ethan Wagner Beady was named after Wagner, Trista's great-grandpa, and after Jared's great-grandfather Ethan. Ethan was the firstborn after Wagner went home to be with the Lord. Mary found comfort each time she held Ethan. Now he was six years old and somehow knew he was extra special to Meemaw. She never had favorites, but Ethan came after Wagner passed. It was just a timely connection for Mary. One thing about being called Meemaw, there was no rank in the name. She was Meemaw equally to all generations of her grandchildren.

Jared, Trista's husband, entered, carrying another two-liter bottle of soda. Ethan followed behind with the final bottle. They both set them on the table near the other bottles.

"What a variety," Meemaw said as she hugged Ethan, who had his arms wrapped around her.

The children went into the living room, where Neil and Jared sat and talked while Trista was giving Winston special attention. He was now an eight-year-old Rottweiler who was Trista's best friend for her first couple of years when she moved in with Jandra. Trista was so glad her grandma let Winston live with her when she got married and had her children. But now, he stays more at Jandra's house than at Trista's. They live next door, so Winston occasionally visits. He likes hanging out with Brucy, Jandra's now nine-and-a-half-year-old Saint Bernard, ever since Admiral, the Doberman Pincher, died from a brain tumor when he turned ten years old. Brucy and Winston stay near Jandra ever since Admiral passed. They haven't left her side since. Jandra thought about getting another dog but hadn't made a decision on that yet.

Doug and Abby arrived with Trent and Paisley. They entered through the front door into the living room. The three women in the kitchen heard the voices of the others growing louder each moment, so they peeked in to see what the commotion was all about.

"Hello, everyone!" Jandra hollered out then went back into the kitchen to gather plates to set up on her dining room table.

"Hi, Mom, do you need help setting up?" Abby asked.

"Everything is about done. I just need cups with ice so drinks can be served," Jandra said gracefully, smiling that her daughter asked. It wasn't too long ago that Abby wouldn't talk to her mother. Now Abby and Jandra talk nearly every day and have a restored relationship that Jandra credits to the Lord.

It wasn't much longer until Jandra announced that dinner was ready. She set the table for eight and the smaller table for four. Paisley asked to sit with her nieces and nephew. She didn't mind that she was six years older than Ethan and eight years older than the twins. She loved being their aunt, yet still so close in age.

Chips and salsa were on each table, food and drinks were served, and everyone talked and ate throughout the dinner. Finishing up before dessert, the younger children and Paisley went in the other room to play while the women cleaned up the dinner dishes to prepare for dessert. Mary was making coffee while Jandra got the dessert plates out of the cupboard. Abby finished loading the dishwasher while making sure there'd be room for the dessert dishes later. The three women sat down and joined in on the conversation at the table.

"Grandma, I'm very thankful you had this dinner. I especially thank you for the Mexican food. You know I love your enchiladas," Trent showered his grandma with praise.

"Of course, I knew what your favorite is. But most of all, it's because I love you so much, and I'm so proud of you that I wanted to have the family together to pray a blessing over you before you leave," Jandra smiled as she hugged her grandson.

"We know you are called by the Lord, Trent. Like your great-grandpa Wagner always said about you, you are going to do great things in Jesus's name. We're all so proud of you," Meemaw said.

"Thanks, Meemaw," Trent said, a little choked up. They all continued talking and asking Trent questions he couldn't quite answer yet.

Before the evening ended, they all held hands and Meemaw prayed a blessing over Trent. She asked the Lord to keep the team safe, to use Trent to reach lost souls in Ethiopia, to bring them all home safely, and to bless and keep Trent in ways only He could do. They all took turns hugging Trent and saying their own individual goodbyes.

Jandra was the last one to hug Trent goodbye. She looked Trent directly in the eyes and said, "You are a special young man. I know God has His hand and favor upon you. I believe God has a special purpose for you in Ethiopia. I will be praying for you daily until you return. This is not a goodbye; this is a send-off with my faith saying, see you soon!" Trent hugged his grandma real tight then let a tear fall down his cheek.

Abby was the first to wake up. She walked into the kitchen and put on a pot of coffee. She grabbed her Bible and opened it to her bookmark in the book of Proverbs. She tried to read a chapter each day first thing in the morning. Her women's Bible study leader had suggested that the ladies did that as a morning routine, like one does when having that first cup of coffee.

Today was Proverbs 31. It was also the day Trent would leave for his mission trip. Abby felt as if she wasn't really reading to be fed but just going through the motions. Her eyes landed on verse nine. She read it over and over and couldn't move past it. "Open your mouth, judge righteously, and plead the cause of the poor and needy." The fourth time she read the verse, she felt tears welling up in her eyes.

"Lord, I don't understand a lot of what I read, but I believe the Bible is Your Word, and You speak to us through it. Trent is leaving today to plead the cause of the poor and needy in Ethiopia. Many are poor in spirit and need You. Why You are calling my son to go there is beyond me, but I am going to make a conscious decision to trust You with him. Trent's excited, and I am afraid. Obviously, I am the one in need of Your help. Help me to stay in confident faith that this is Your plan for Trent," she prayed.

Abby continued to read through the chapter, then flipped her pages back to place her bookmark in chapter one to prepare it for tomorrow's reading. She flipped a little too far back and landed on Psalm chapter one-twenty-one. She noticed she had highlighted verses one and two that read, "I will lift up my eyes to the hills—From whence comes my help? My help comes from the Lord, Who made heaven and earth."

Abby exhaled a heavy sigh then smiled as she looked up toward heaven. She knew that was her answer from God. Of course, He would help her. She closed her Bible and stood up to poor herself a cup of freshly brewed coffee. Doug walked in and put his arms around Abby.

"Today's the day," he whispered.

"It sure is," Abby replied.

"Trent's going to be fine," Doug said as he reached around her to grab a coffee cup.

"Yes, I know," she smiled and kissed Doug's cheek.

"Morning," Trent's voice pierced the quietness of their whispers.

"Good morning. Did you finish your packing last night?" Abby asked.

"Yes, Mom, and I slept really good," he replied, answering the potential next question.

"Let me make you a good sendoff breakfast. What would you like?" Abby asked.

"I'll just have a bowl of cereal and a banana. I'm too excited to eat," Trent answered.

"Okay, then I'll pack you a bag of snacks for the plane ride," Abby stated as she found a bag he could put in his backpack. Everyone going on the trip was told they could bring one large suitcase to be checked in and one carry-on for computers, their Bible, and other small items. They were also allowed a small backpack to have at their seats. That was where this bag of snacks would go, along with his cell phone, charger, passport, and wallet.

Paisley was the last to get up, and she quickly put on a pair of sweats and tennis shoes. She said she'd eat later when they came back from dropping Trent off at the airport.

Making sure Trent had everything, they loaded Doug's truck and proceeded to the airport. Abby was silent but still in a warm mood. Doug was reminding Trent to take a lot of pictures and to write or call whenever he could. Abby had bought Trent a stationary package and gave him ten books of stamps so he could write often to them.

At the airport, they could only go as far as the drop-off area, which was full of other families dropping off their children. They saw Pastor Mauer and parked the truck to unload Trent's luggage. Before Trent walked away, Abby asked another parent to take a photo of the four of them on her cell phone.

"We love you, Trent. Stay safe and know you are in our prayers," Abby said, hugging her son tightly.

"I love you too, Mom," Trent said, then hugged Doug saying the same.

"I'll actually miss you," Paisley said as she hugged Trent tight.

"I'll miss you more than you know. Take care of Mom," Trent whispered in his younger sister's ear.

"Okay," she said tearfully.

Trent started walking toward the mission team group. They noticed a friend of Trent's approaching him, and the two young men shook hands and walked together. Abby, Doug, and Paisley all yelled out loudly that they loved him. Trent turned around, touched his heart, smiled, and waved goodbye.

Abby, Doug, and Paisley drove home in silence. Once home, they all stood on the front porch looking into the sky, wondering if the plane they saw high up in the distance was Trent's plane. It was probably too soon, but they all waved as if it was.

"God bless and protect them all," Doug said.

CHAPTER THREE

After the mission team took roll call, Pastor Mauer and his assistants handed out dark green T-shirts that read "Team Jesus" for everyone to put on over their clothes. It was a way to recognize everyone on their team at a quick glance. There were sixteen teenagers, three assistant pastors, and Pastor Mauer. It was a team group of twenty total. An airport employee took several photos of the group together for them.

Once they were all checked in, they boarded the large airplane. Before they took off, Pastor Mauer said a prayer for safe travels, favor on God's children to lead the Ethiopians to Christ to obtain salvation, and that God's mercy and grace would go before them. He closed his prayer by asking the Holy Spirit to be with them each step of this journey. They all unanimously hollered out with loud whoo-hoo's and whistling, then said collectively, "In Jesus' name, Amen!"

The airline flight attendant came out to announce it was time to buckle up; she explained the safety issues and that they would arrive in Addis Ababa, Ethiopia in Africa, in approximately a little over twenty-two hours. The team looked at each other with saucer size excited eyes and grins. They were told to stay buckled up in their seats until the fasten seat belt sign turned off. She stated once safe, she and the other flight attendants would come around to bring drinks, snacks and help with any questions.

The rumbling of the plane grew louder, and the speed for takeoff thrust them all back in their seats. Trent and his buddy Dylan sat together near the window seat. This Boeing 747 was a jumbo widespread aircraft, with two aisles and seven seats per row. Two by the window on either side and three seats in the middle. They were happy about the window view.

Once they were allowed to walk around, Trent went over to Pastor Mauer and thanked him for this opportunity. Pastor Mauer stood up and told his team to start calling him Pastor Rick. It was more personable, and he wanted the youth to consider him more as a friend than an authority.

As the hours passed by, little by little, eyes were closing, and sleep was arriving. Trent's friend Dylan drifted off, so Trent turned on his overhead light and pulled out his Bible. He had kept his Bible in his backpack along with the special snacks his mom packed. Abby had packed a small bag of homemade cookies which Trent was nibbling on. He prayed quietly to himself and thanked the Lord for trusting him to minister to a foreign country.

Trent opened his Bible to the Book of Psalms and started reading. He often stopped to memorize Scripture. He learned that memorizing a verse was a form of meditating on it. He knew Psalm 1 by heart, so after he recited it by memory, he began Psalm 2. It was verse eight that caught his attention. "Ask of Me, and I will give You the nations for Your inheritance, and the ends of the earth for Your possession."

He started reading his Bible's study notes and realized verses six through nine were about Jesus. Then Trent looked at Matthew 28:16–20 and saw how the resurrected Jesus gave what we know as the Great Commission. Jesus knew He had the authority in heaven and earth and sent His disciples out to make disciples in other nations.

Trent closed his eyes and thought about it all. Jesus was sending Trent out with authority in His name to make disciples in Ethiopia. Trent's desire instantly changed from just reaching the lost to baptizing them and making disciples so they could carry on in Ethiopia the call of the Lord. Trent sat up straight and asked the Lord *what His calling on Trent's life really was?*

"What's going on, Lord? Am I a missionary or what?" Trent asked silently in his heart.

"My son, you are on a mission trip with a special purpose. I have called you to tell others about Jesus, that you know. You have been given the gift of an evangelist, but first, I have to send you on a mission. Do not worry. You are right where I need you to be." The voice wasn't audible to others, but Trent knew he heard from God.

Not knowing what to do next, Trent wondered if he should wake up Dylan and tell him. Should he wake up Pastor Rick and tell him what just happened? Trent was so excited that God revealed something very specific to him that he was bursting to tell someone. No one on his team was awake, so Trent just ate another one of his mom's home-baked chocolate chip cookies. The flight attendant came over to Trent and offered him a neck pillow. He thanked her and put it around his neck. Swallowing the last bite of his cookie, he leaned his seat back and closed his eyes. Right before falling asleep, Trent thought, *That was a good cookie.*

Arriving at the Bole International Airport in Addis Ababa, Ethiopia, Trent was fascinated by the obvious cultural differences and the similarities. The people dressed differently—that was obvious. They spoke differently and played Ethiopian music across the speakers, yet the shops and food courts in the airport were similar to USA airports. The food and clothing stores were very similar. There were signs of coffee, burgers, and even M&M candy posters that were displayed. Most of all, the smell of coffee and fresh-baked pastries was so strong that most of the team stopped to buy something. Everyone seemed impressed at the stores and wondered if this was how it was in the cities.

An old large church bus was waiting to pick up this mission team and drive them to their hotel. It was very weathered looking with faded colors and chipped paint. A young dark-skinned man dressed in an orange T-shirt and baggie white gauze-looking pants met them with a sign he held up that read: Oregon USA Pastor Rick team. The group quickly loaded their luggage and couldn't help but smile at the man whose contagious smile welcomed them. He would greet each person by saying, "Tadias, Ibalalew Amadi. Which is to say, "Hello, my name is Amadi."

Everyone smiled and said in return, "Tadias."

Once on the bus, Amadi spoke fairly good English. He explained that he was their travel guide sent from the church of missions. He explained that he was their designated driver to transport them to their destination. He did his best to answer any questions. The young people took many pictures of the surrounding area. It looked like it was a popular city. The hotel was a temporary stop. Just two nights there, probably for the team to get their bearings after the long flight. The hotel was quite nice. It was a typical Best Western hotel. Everyone was able to sleep, eat, shower, and prepare for their fifteen-hour journey by bus in two days. They would be staying in a local village in a town called Ambo. Ambo was fairly safe and known for its mineral water. They would be just outside of Aksum near Tigray, which is a region in Hawzen Woreda. It was a dangerous place not long ago, probably still is. They will visit the newer restored church called St. Mary of Zion Christian Church. It is believed to have once housed the Ark of the Covenant. Some believe it still does.

After their stay in the hotel, they were packed up and ready to drive the course to their destination. Pastor Rick's friend, Kojo Hailu, or Pastor Jo as he liked to be called, would take over as their main guide, with Amadi as his helper.

Pastor Rick told the team that Pastor Jo lived in Ethiopia but that they met during a Christian conference in Portland, Oregon, many years ago and have been friends ever since. Pastor Jo once attended and helped in maintenance at the Ethiopian Evangelical Church in Portland, Oregon. He has since moved back to Ethiopia to help build new Christian churches and to use his small village to host and house traveling missionaries.

The drive was a little rough. There were no real paved roads. As they drove, they would spot children walking with dogs and an occasional goat. Some didn't wear shoes, and their clothes showed signs of filth and wear. But they seemed to be smiling and playing as most children do. Occasionally, they'd see young men and teenage boys riding very old-looking, rusted bicycles, but mainly people walked. The boys and young men mainly wore long sleeve tunic shirts that hung down to their knees and gauze-looking pants. Only children could wear shorts. It wasn't showing maturity if shorts were worn.

The women walked in long skirts with what looked like home-made weaved bowls or baskets on their heads. Others wore long woven bags hanging on their sides and a baby strapped to either their backs or their chest. Their poverty could be felt by all. They later learned that this wasn't even the poorest area. It was quite humbling, to say the least.

Some of the people bore darker skin tones than others, and the girls on the bus wondered if it was because they were out in the sun longer or genetics. Most were dark, black-skinned, while others were a brown tanned color. Trent looked on, thinking about Rusty's comments. He found a deeper resentment for Rusty growing. Trent saw all of these people, and his heart was telling him they were all children of God who needed to meet their Father.

It was a beautiful warm summer morning as Jandra drank her morning cup of coffee as she sat on her favorite bench outback. She listened to the loud squawks of the blue jays fighting over the birdseed. Neil obviously filled up the bird feeder that stood on the tall wooden stand.

She smiled as she thought of Trent being across the world on a different continent. She knew Africa was about ten hours ahead of USA time. She said a quick prayer asking God to give Trent and the team special favor there in Ethiopia. Jandra remembered how Trent told her God talked to him at such a young age. Jandra knew from the first time Trent mentioned God, having never been to church, that he was attuned to Him and that he would be used by God. Going to Africa surprised most, but not Jandra.

A few moments later, Mary came out carrying her Bible and cup of tea. She took a deep breath and exhaled loudly.

"Good morning, Mom. Why the big sigh?" Jandra asked.

"I wasn't sighing; I was exhaling all of yesterday's troubles out of my mind, making room for what today holds," Mary answered.

"Dad used to say that," Jandra said.

"He got that from me," Mary teased and grinned.

"I miss Dad," Jandra admitted.

"I do too. Some days more than others. But it won't be much longer, and we'll all be together," Mary smiled at her daughter.

The two women sat in silence as they each contemplated Mary's last comment. In the distance, they heard the sound of Neil's quad runner making its way toward their house. As he pulled up, both women greeted him with a smile and cursory good morning.

"There's coffee in the pot," Jandra said.

"No time this morning. I have a few errands I have to run before my dinner date this evening," Neil stated.

"Dinner date? With who?" Jandra asked, taken aback by his announcement.

"Debbie Johnson from the church," he answered. Neil knew this would come as a surprise to Jandra, as he never mentioned any interest in Debbie.

"I didn't realize you were interested in Debbie," Jandra stated the obvious.

"It's Debbie who showed an interest in me. She asked me out to dinner," he explained, knowing he didn't owe Jandra an explanation but offered one anyway.

"Why did you come down here? To gloat?" she asked.

"No. To ask if you ladies needed anything from the market. That'll be my last stop," he offered.

"No, thank you," Mary answered.

"Nope. I don't need anything," Jandra replied, then stood up to return to her house.

"Okay then, I'll be going," Neil said as he started the quad. He and Jandra had been very close friends for years. He told her everything. He also realized that's all they were and ever been—just friends.

Jandra felt her stomach tighten with the news of Neil dating. She considered Neil her best friend. She also assumed, in an unspoken way deep down, they were more than just friends. Now she understood that was *her* assumption. In the kitchen, Jandra rinsed out her coffee cup then stood holding the edge of the sink.

"Lord, what's happening?" she asked as she heard her mother come inside.

"Are you okay, Jandra?" Mary asked.

"I have to be. I guess I always thought of Neil as *my* friend, not anyone else's," Jandra admitted.

"I admit I'm a little surprised, too. I really believed you two would quit claiming you're *just friends* and drop your intimacy barriers and join forces," Mary stated.

"What do you mean?" Jandra asked.

"We all know how close you two are and always wondered why you didn't take the next step," she explained.

"What's the next step, Mom?" Jandra inquired.

"That you two would make your closeness official by dating each other. Your love for each other is evident," Mary further explained.

"Evident to who?" Jandra asked.

"To all who see you two together," Mary said, then rinsed her cup and proceeded to her room.

"I thought so, too. Lord, I thought so, too," she whispered and swallowed hard.

The rest of the day was a blur to Jandra. Deep down, she knew she missed her opportunity somehow. She really did love and care for Neil, but at this moment, she resented him. He didn't say he was lonely and wanted to start dating. Why didn't he reach out to Jandra? Why Debbie Johnson?

About an hour later, Trista came over with the kids. Ethan immediately hugged his great-grandma then asked where Meemaw was. He and Meemaw had a special connection.

"Hi, Grandma," Trista said to Jandra while giving her a kiss on the cheek.

"Hi, Trista," she responded.

"Grandma, what's wrong?" her granddaughter asked, always aware of her demeanor.

Jandra told her about Neil. She tried to minimize her feelings by saying it's okay, they are just friends after all. Trista didn't buy it but didn't want to push things and upset her grandma.

"Grandma, Audrey, and I have a speaking engagement today. Would you watch the kids until Jared gets home from work?" Trista asked.

"Of course, I will. Where are you two speaking today?" Jandra asked, half interested.

"We're going to Medford to be guest speakers at a rape survivor's convention. Audrey will drop off her daughter Amy, is that okay?" Trista's eyes pleaded.

"That's fine," Jandra replied. She loved Audrey and Amy like her own granddaughters and loved the fact that Amy was about three or more years older than Ethan. That gave Ethan someone else to play with, besides his younger twin sisters, Hannah and Sarah. They still took naps, and he didn't think he needed to anymore.

Audrey came to pick Trista up and drop Amy off. The two young ladies went to fulfill their commitment, and Mary entered the living room with her three great-great-grandchildren following her closely.

"Hi Meemaw," Amy said as she hugged Mary. Everyone knew Mary as Meemaw, and she loved it.

"Hello, Amy. It seems we're having a busy day," Mary winked at Jandra.

"It seems so," Jandra smiled, happy to be distracted from her thoughts of Neil.

It wasn't long before the kids were picked up, and her house was quiet again. Jandra was climbing into bed when her thoughts went back to Neil, and she began praying.

"Lord, I'm confused. I figured Neil would grow old with me. Now I realize You must have different plans for him. You know I don't want to grow old alone. So, what do I do now? I don't like this feeling. Am I jealous?" Jandra asked as she prayed.

"Are you?" an inner voice in her spirit asked.

CHAPTER FOUR

Trent and the team arrived safely. There were small hut-looking rooms that held three people comfortably. Each hut had three beds, three small makeshift dressers with three small drawers in each. A make-shift toilet area and bathtub with a curtain around it for privacy.

Pastor Rick and the three assistant pastors would stay in Pastor Jo's small home. It was an old hut that was extended to hold more rooms, made with thin steel frames that had wood and fiber mixed with cement for strength. The other huts were made of the same, but many had cracked walls and rooves. The girls were more concerned about their lodging than the boys were. But overall, they knew they would have to endure hard conditions when signing up.

Trent, Dylan, and a young man named Bret chose to live together. They would live there for five months and would periodically go on special treks to different locations to share the Gospel of Jesus Christ. Trent took numerous pictures of his hut, his surroundings, and selfies of him and his friends. He even snapped a photo of the old bus and Amadi.

Once settled, the team would begin walking to a closely located village where actual Ethiopian, born and raised, citizens lived. Not a missionary team from another country. They were aware that missionary groups periodically stayed in Pastor Jo's village. They were not the first team. But they were excited as if they were. They had about a two-mile walk in the heat to the little village. It was there that they would join the Ethiopian missionaries to plan a small trek together.

Trent couldn't tell at face value if anyone felt as excited as he did. His friend Dylan was eager to go somewhere, but even Dylan didn't know where. He just needed to be on the move. Trent admired Dylan's spunk but was more interested in Dylan's true desire. Trent summed up Dylan as an adventurous sort.

They all made it to the next village and were greeted by a fairly small group consisting of about ten or twelve young guys and gals. Trent looked around, surveying the people. He noticed a group of three girls about his age. Each wearing the traditional long skirt and a colored T-shirt. The color of their shirts was different on each girl. He heard someone hollering toward the three girls.

"Binta, Binta!" an older lady yelled out.

"Ow!" the bronzed-skinned girl in a fuchsia T-shirt with her hair pulled up in a ponytail hollered in response.

The elderly lady handed her something. Trent couldn't make out what it was, but he heard the girl reply, "Ameseginalehu." He recognized the word from his bus driver, Amadi, to mean *thank you*.

The girl put whatever she was given into a small bag that she was carrying. She raised her head up and saw Trent staring at her. She smiled as they locked eyes. Trent smiled back. He heard Pastor Rick calling for the team to gather. Trent turned to walk towards Pastor Rick and the others. With the girl's smile still flooding his mind, Trent looked back to see her still watching him and smiling. Trent blushed, then turned around and said out loud yet to himself, "Who was that girl, and what's a Binta?"

It was the third day that Trent would wake up to the strange smell of breakfast. He learned his breakfast was known as Fir-Fir, which was basically leftover Injera, which was a fermented flat bread that had a spongy texture. It was stir-fried with Berbere, a very spicy hot spice, and Shiro, a powdered chickpea bean meal with garlic and onions. Sometimes they used Kibbe, which was ground lamb. It wasn't his favorite, that's for sure. It was breakfast time that he missed his mom's or grandma's bacon and eggs.

Dylan enjoyed it, but he enjoyed anything that he could chew and swallow. Trent figured he'd learn to like the food, or he'd lose a lot of weight and merely starve. Trent did find there is quite a bit of various fruits and vegetables that grow easily there. Avocados, papayas, bananas, and asparagus, which Trent enjoyed, were readily available. He wouldn't starve after all, but he'd probably end up a vegetarian. He also brought ten Brita water filter straws to aid with his drinking the underground well water. Trent would be okay.

After breakfast time and prayer, the group was going to St. Mary of Zion Church. The ministers there would give a potential list and map of areas to reach out to. Trent made sure he had his cell phone for pictures. He knew his battery would be low soon, so he was very frugal on his photo taking.

His dad gave him four battery-operated chargers that he would use sparingly. He knew getting pictures of this church would mean a lot to his grandma. When it came to Christian issues, structures, and any Christian beliefs read about only, his grandmother Jandra would love to see all he could show her.

Neil had gotten home late after his dinner with Debbie the other night. After picking Debbie up at her house, Neil had driven to a Chinese restaurant that she chose. It was fairly nice. He noticed Debbie had a lot of saké. Neil didn't drink alcohol and was surprised at the amount Debbie did: a lot. He made a mental note of that and did his best to enjoy his dinner. When the check came, things got awkward.

"Since I asked you out, I guess I will pay," Debbie slightly slurred.

"I'll tell you what, we'll go Dutch," Neil replied and was grateful the conversation went this way. Her half of the bill was three times as much as his from her multiple drinks alone.

"Neil, I was being nice, I assumed as the man you would pay," her slurring getting worse.

"You know what they say about assuming," he answered.

He asked the waiter if he could give them separate checks. He didn't want any more confusion. Once the waiter returned with their checks, they proceeded to the cashier to pay. Debbie grabbed Neil's arm to help steady her walk. Neil was feeling a little embarrassed by Debbie's physical demeanor. He helped her to his truck and proceeded to the driver's door.

"Neil, aren't you going to open the door for me and help me in?" Debbie pouted.

"The door's unlocked," he said, regretting that he went out with her.

"But I can't get in. I need your strong arms to help lift me up," she said as she batted her eyelashes.

Neil went around and opened the passenger door and grabbed the top of her left arm to steady her.

"Neil, honey, you do realize this is a date, and you will be rewarded if you treat me like your special lady," she said as she grabbed the seatbelt and buckled in.

"Debbie, I don't know if you'll remember this tomorrow or not, but you're not my special lady. I think of you as a Christian sister, maybe even a friend. But I'm not ready to date in hopes of finding my special lady. Do you understand?" he firmly asked.

"Sure," she slurred. Then she continued, "But I can make you happy and make you forget about Jandra," she said with half-opened eyelids now.

"What in the world does Jandra have to do with this?" he asked calmly.

"I've seen you two together for years. I've never seen you intimate with each other. When asked, you both say you're just friends. I figured since you agreed to go out with me, you wanted more from a woman. And I'm willing to give you more," she teased as she lowered the zipper on her blouse.

Debbie was a very attractive woman physically. She had all of the right curves and a beautiful smile that drew you into her mouth that was usually outlined with red lipstick on her lips. She usually came across as a sweet, polite Christian woman. Always volunteering at church, always laughing at the men's jokes, and she managed to touch the closest man's bicep whenever she was talking. She was alluring, and for a Christian man, very dangerous.

Neil pulled up to her house then exited his truck. He went around to the passenger side and helped Debbie out, then escorted her to the front door.

"Do you want to come inside for a nightcap?" she wobbled and slurred.

"Absolutely not. I don't think you need a nightcap anyway," he said as she unlocked her front door and stepped inside.

"You'll regret this, Neil! I'm the best there is," she hollered as Neil walked down her driveway, got into his truck, and started it up to leave.

Neil drove toward his home but stopped at a little park near a creak. It was late and dark, but he used his cell phone to read Proverbs chapters five through seven. It was about immoral women, adultery, and harlots. He wasn't saying Debbie Johnson was a harlot, but she had a Jezebel spirit on her, and Neil wanted no part of that.

He asked the Lord what was happening in his life. Was he lonely and seeking a woman's companionship? Then he answered his own concern by realizing he does have companionship with Jandra. He must be desiring more. But does he want more from Jandra, or is he ready to find a wife to fulfill all of his needs? He was confused.

"Lord, what's wrong with me? Am I so shallow that I'm searching for a woman who poses as God's gift to men?" he asked out loud in the quiet of his truck cab. He laughed as he said that. There's no such thing as God's gift of *one woman to men*. He changed his focus and prayed out loud to God, "Father, there's a woman who is your gift for *me*. Open my eyes so I can find her."

CHAPTER FIVE

Pastor Rick and Pastor Jo led the way to the church. Upon arrival, Trent noticed several stone structures. It was a sacred place, to say the least. Trent snapped photos of everything he could. He spun around to his right to capture some stone pillars that looked ancient when he noticed the Ethiopian girl in the fuchsia T-shirt. Without thinking, he snapped her photo. He lowered his cell phone and caught her smiling at him.

She walked closer to Trent and stopped. Smiling, he gave an awkward wave as if to gesture a greeting of hello.

"Hello," her soft voice came.

"Hello. Do you speak English?" Trent asked.

"Yes," the bronze girl giggled.

"I'm Trent," he introduced himself while touching his chest.

"I'm Binta," she responded back, giggling with the same hand-to-chest gesture.

"Your name is Binta," he stated as if a lightbulb went off in his head.

"And your name is Trent," she returned the statement as if this was some sort of ritual.

"Right," he giggled. He looked at this young girl and noticed she had golden, olive color eyes. They were not the normal dark brown like the others.

"You have really pretty eyes," Trent said.

"Like my father," she blurted.

"I have eyes like me," Trent said, causing Binta to giggle.

"You're funny," she stated.

"How do you speak English so well?" Trent wondered out loud.

"My father was an American and taught me," she explained.

"Oh. What is he now, Ethiopian?" Trent asked.

"He's dead," she stated.

"Oh, I'm sorry, Binta," Trent said humbly and wanted to quickly change the subject.

"He and my mother were killed by the Ethiopian government when the TPLF attacked a military base, causing the government to strike back and kill tens of thousands from Amhara region, as sponsored militiamen who were committed to an *ethnic cleansing* operation," she coldly stated.

"Whoa. I never heard of such a thing. What is TPLF?" he asked innocently ignorant.

"Tigray People's Liberation Front," Binta explained.

"Oh. Binta, I'm so sorry about your parents," Trent realized he had opened a conversation that he knew nothing about.

Binta knew he was uncomfortable talking about this, so she quickly changed the subject and refocused their attention to their united missionary goal.

"Are you a missionary for our Lord Jesus?" she asked with that smile that caught Trent's attention.

"Yes, Binta, I am. I actually believe the Lord is calling me to be an Evangelist," he told her, realizing he hadn't really told anyone else.

"That's nice. I don't really know my purpose yet. Maybe a missionary, maybe a teacher, maybe a mother someday; I don't really know," Binta said, shrugging her shoulders.

"A teacher? That's a big purpose," Trent stated.

"I studied at the Axum University for nearly two years after they rebuilt. They built an entire University after the November 2020 massacre. It took about four years to reopen, but I enrolled and studied for close to two years. I graduated with an Associate's Degree in teaching, but I couldn't afford to enroll the extra years for a Bachelor's and ultimately a Master's Degree. I was funded for the Associate's Degree as a child of multiple family murder victims. Actually, they refer to me as a militiamen victim, but I call it murder," she shared it all without blinking an eye.

"May I ask you how old you are?" Trent asked. He didn't think she was old enough to have gone to college.

"I am twenty-two. How old are you?" Binta replied.

"Really? You look younger than me. I'm nineteen," Trent responded.

"My mother was three years older than my father. It must be a good sign," Binta smiled.

Trent heard the pastors calling their teams. Having to leave, Trent hugged Binta very tightly and close to him. He felt an involuntary response to what Binta was sharing about her life. He whispered in her ear that they would talk more soon. Binta held both of Trent's upper arms and surprisingly said, "Yes, Trent, we will."

Returning to their prospective teams, they each were given a list and map to nearby villages. Trent's team went left, and Binta's team went right. Dylan hurried to get next to Trent.

"I saw you with that girl," Dylan chided.

"And? So?" Trent said a little defensively.

"So, nothing. I was just saying I saw you," Dylan tried to backtrack.

"We're not in second grade; I can talk to a girl," Trent said.

"I know. But dude, you found a girl. I can't even find a goat around here," Dylan tried to be funny.

"I didn't realize you were looking for a goat," Trent punched his friend in the arm then laughed.

After walking about three miles, the two boys were silenced when they entered the small village. This was serious poverty. Pastor Jo led the way to the center of the village and, in a loud voice, yelled out, "Envoys will come out of Egypt; Ethiopia will quickly stretch out her hands to God!"

Many villagers came near to assess the situation. Pastor Jo explained to his team that most could understand English. He told them he was quoting Psalm 68:31 and that God Almighty loved the Ethiopians and wanted them to trust Him. He then sent the team out two members each. They had prepared on how to initiate telling them about the Gospel of Jesus Christ.

They were teamed up, one male and one female. Trent was teamed up with a fellow church girl named Veronica. She was very passionate about Jesus, and Trent loved the fact he would witness with her.

"Tadias," Veronica greeted a small family consisting of an older man, an older woman, and three teenage boys.

"Tadias," the group replied.

"We want to tell you the good news of Jesus Christ," Trent began.

They were able to quote Scripture to this family and tell them how their sins are forgiven through the shed Blood of Jesus and how they can receive everything Christ paid for them to have simply by believing.

By the end of their conversation, all five members of that family proclaimed their belief that Jesus is the Son of God, and they all said the sinner's prayer and invited Jesus into their hearts. Veronica prayed they would receive the Holy Spirit, and Pastor Rick told each group they could go to the nearby mucky water hole, and he and Pastor Jo would be there to baptize any who wanted to be baptized.

The three associate pastors walked around helping any who were having trouble. Dylan and his partner, Ruby, were having trouble answering questions. They all were reminded this was about sharing what they knew about Jesus, not trying to be theologians.

Trent and Veronica stepped into the dirty water to assist. They were both on cloud nine when the team headed back to their village. They sang in unison, This Is the Day, an old Sunday school song taken from Psalm 118:24.

Back in their huts, after getting cleaned up and getting ready for bed, Trent conversed out loud with his two roommates.

"This was an exciting experience," Trent said.

"It sure was. Did Pastor Rick say how many were saved?" Bret asked.

"I think he said about forty," Trent answered.

"I had a hard time," Dylan admitted.

"Why? It was easy," Bret said arrogantly.

"Ruby and I didn't click, and we couldn't remember anything," Dylan confessed.

"There was a cheat sheet you could follow if you don't know what to say or do," Bret said.

The tension between the two boys was heating up; Trent recognized the pride in both boys. Bret bragged in pride, and Dylan was a failure in his pride. Trent interrupted the two by standing in between them.

"Knock it off! This isn't about who is better than the other; this is about Jesus and the lost. That spirit of pride on both of you is not welcome here. Bret, you think you know everything, and Dylan, you feel your pride is hurt. It's not about either of you. You're both sent to share the Gospel of Jesus Christ, not the gospel of Bret or Dylan. Check your motives," Trent said and then suggested they pray. The two young men first stood with their heads down as if they were reprimanded by a parent. Then the three of them held hands in agreement while Trent prayed.

"Father, we praise You for a great day. We thank You for using us. We glorify You for drawing our new brothers and sisters to You. Forgive us for being prideful. Forgive our personal arrogance. Forgive our feeling worthless. Keep us from Satan's attacks and revive our purpose to bring You all of the glory. Remove any form of anger from this hut and our team collectively. Holy Spirit, teach us what to say to reach those who need a word from God. In Jesus's name, amen."

Bret and Dylan simultaneously said amen, then the three boys quietly got into their cots. Several minutes later, you could hear the rustling of bedding.

"Dude, where did you learn to pray like that?" Dylan asked Trent.

"I didn't learn. I was just talking to my Father," Trent replied and closed his eyes, smiling really big in the darkness. His mind was remembering all of the day's events. All of them.

Neil was contemplating his arrival at Jandra's as he walked towards her house. Would she interrogate him about his date with Debbie the other night? He knew he couldn't just avoid Jandra forever. It had been two and a half days already. She was his best friend, after all. He played it normal and opened her kitchen door.

"Good morning, Mary," he said as he entered and noticed Mary was sitting at the table drinking her coffee alone.

"Good morning," she responded with a smile. She then got up and poured Neil a cup of coffee and handed it to him.

"Where's Jandra?" he asked.

"Probably in the bedroom. She'll be out in a moment," Mary stated.

Neil couldn't read the atmosphere with Mary. He was smart not to volunteer information. He knew that would only make him look guilty of something. He would wait for someone to question him. It was wise to honestly answer a question than to just blurt out a senseless defense. He wasn't guilty of anything, yet he felt he owed them an explanation of his taking Debbie Johnson out to dinner. But he would wait.

"Good morning, Neil," came Jandra's normal greeting.

"Good morning. I noticed the animals were fed," he said.

"I was up early, so I went ahead and fed them," she replied. She hoped she would be kind and not sarcastic to Neil. She knew the Lord would want her to have gentle, quiet understanding. Something God has been working on Jandra for years about. She had a tendency to just blurt out words that did more harm than good.

"I guess I overslept a bit today. I've been busy feeding the homeless the past two days," he confessed and volunteering his whereabouts.

Jandra wasn't going to play the jealousy game she knew Satan was tempting her with. Mary recognized Jandra's pursed lips and decided she'd break the ice before her daughter said something foolish that she'd later regret.

"How was your date the other night?" she asked gently like a concerned mother.

"It really wasn't a date. It was just dinner," Neil began, then he added, "it wasn't great."

"Where'd you go?" Jandra asked calmly.

"To that Chinese place near Albertson's," Neil stated.

"How was the food there?" Mary questioned.

"I guess it was okay. I'm not a Chinese food kind of guy," he smiled.

"Then why'd you go?" Jandra asked.

"Debbie chose the place. I just drove," he explained.

"Did she like it?" Jandra asked, knowing she was starting to cross the nosey line.

"I guess," Neil replied.

"What did you do afterward?" Jandra started to sound like a drill sergeant.

"Nothing," he said.

Knowing Neil was a man of few words, she decided to back off. She trusted her friend to make smart choices. She also knew the Lord would not condone her personal interrogation or jealousy. Neil was a smart man and didn't owe Jandra a play-by-play of his evening.

"I'm sorry, Neil. I'm acting nosey," Jandra stated.

"You're acting jealous," Mary confronted the obvious.

"Mom," Jandra sounded irritated.

"This silly line of questioning could go on all day. I believe Jandra was surprised you went out with Debbie, and she got her feelings hurt that you didn't tell her. You two have been friends for years, and neither of you has dated anyone else. This was a shock to her," Mary said, defending her daughter yet revealing Jandra's truth.

"I understand. I wasn't dating Debbie. I took her to dinner because she asked me to go. Turns out she drinks too much, so we parted our ways after we ate," Neil gave Jandra just enough information to satisfy her inquiring mind.

"I'm not jealous, and I wasn't asking," Jandra said and realized she should say no more.

"Okay," was all Neil said.

They all finished their coffee, and Neil excused himself to run a few errands. Mary and Jandra began straightening up the kitchen.

"Mom, why did you say all of that?" Jandra asked.

"Because it's true. You two are inseparable, yet you don't allow yourselves to admit your true feelings for each other. I simply stated the obvious," Mary said.

"I don't think he feels that way for me. Plus, I'm not sure if I feel that way for him. I've never dated anyone after Billy died," Jandra stated.

"I know. But Neil is a good man and a better friend to you, and he obviously cares. You two should talk about your relationship. Maybe it's time for him to consider what it would mean to spend his future in this house, rather than his 5th wheel," Mary said all she was going to say.

Mary loved Neil like a son and would love to see him and Jandra happy together. She also knew her daughter, and Jandra was pretty stubborn. Mary knew Jandra was also afraid to get hurt again. What happened with Jandra's husband was beyond devastating for her. Jandra couldn't even grieve for her dying husband because she was falsely accused and arrested for his untimely, senseless death. Jandra had her heart very guarded.

The two ladies parted to their own bedrooms.

Jandra walked into her bedroom and found Goliath lying on her bed. She picked up Goliath, Mary's very large Maine Coon cat. That cat seemed to sense when Jandra needed a friend because he would periodically lay on her bed until she picked him up and cuddled him.

"Goliath, you're a good friend. You're always here when I need you," Jandra whispered as she hugged him.

"So am I," a soft whisper spoke to her spirit.

CHAPTER SIX

Trent woke up early to go with Amadi, Pastor Rick, and a few other members of their team to drive the fifteen-hour drive back to Addis Ababa. They would spend one night in the Best Western hotel then return to their camp near Aksum. They tried to make the trip once a month to pick up any necessary supplies and to mail any letters the group had ready. Pastor Jo had a mailbox in that city specifically for postal communications. By next month's trip, they would have letters from family to pick up. Keeping the group communicating with their families was important. There was a local shop that made photos from cameras and cell phones, so each month, they would have pictures printed up. Trent was excited to send his first letter home and tell them photos would be in next month's letter.

Back in the hotel room, Trent laid on his bed while his hotel roommate, a counselor named Vince, sat in a round chair near the room's only table.

"Vince, can I talk to you about something?" Trent asked.

"Sure, anything," he politely said. Vince was about twenty-nine years old, making him nearly ten years older than Trent.

"Have you ever had a serious girlfriend?" Trent nervously approached the conversation.

"Of course. I have one now back home," he stated.

"I've never really had a serious one. I've gone on a few dates, but nothing serious," Trent admitted.

"Why do you ask?" Vince sensed there was more to this question.

"I guess I'm trying to ask if you've ever been in love?" Trent blurted.

Smiling, Vince guessed the direction this was going. "Are you referring to a special girl I see you spending time with?" Vince turned his chair so he could face Trent.

"Yes, that would be Binta. I really enjoy talking with her and find myself thinking about her when she's not around. I've never felt this way before. Do you think it's because I'm so far away from home and lonely?" Trent genuinely asked.

"Do you think it's because you're so far away from home and lonely?" Vince returned Trent's question.

Trent thought for a moment, then replied, "This may sound crazy, but when I'm with Binta, I feel like I am at home and supposed to be here."

"It sounds serious. Have you told Binta of your feelings?" Vince asked.

"Not entirely. But when I'm with her, it's like words aren't enough. I feel like my heart comes to life when I see her looking at me. I must sound silly," Trent said as he rolled over and groaned.

"You don't sound silly, you sound like Boaz who found his Ruth," Vince grinned.

Trent thought about the story of Boaz being Ruth's kinsman-redeemer. Boaz was a foreshadow of Jesus being our Kinsman-Redeemer. Jesus redeemed us back by paying the price on the cross. Trent read the four chapters of Ruth and felt in his spirit that he was Binta's kinsman-redeemer. Trent believed he was blessed with the duty of restoring the rights to Binta and avenging the wrongs done to her and her family. He also knew it wasn't entirely like Boaz and Ruth, and he knew he wouldn't avenge the wrongs done to her, really, but he would be a type of redeemer to restore love and security to Binta.

Trent learned he needed to pray and seek God when making huge decisions. Actually, Trent learned to seek God even in the small choices he made. He asked the Lord to give him clarity concerning Binta. Then Trent asked the Lord for His favor. Looking at the photo he took of Binta and now having it as an actual, tangible picture, Trent smiled at the image of her smiling face. Trent was dozing off when he thought he heard the Lord whisper to him, "Remember when you asked what a Binta was? Ask Me again."

It was nearly two and a half months since Trent left for Ethiopia. Paisley checked the mailbox at the end of their driveway and found a large manilla envelope addressed to her family with a return address stamped Ethiopia, Africa all over it.

"Mom, Mom!" Paisley hollered.

"What on earth is the matter?" Abby asked loudly as she hurried toward Paisley.

"We have a package from Trent!" Paisley still screamed even though Abby was standing next to her.

"Open it!" Abby yelled excitedly, then said, "No, wait for your dad."

"Where is Dad?" Paisley asked, feeling the weight of the envelope.

"He went to his men's breakfast at church. He should be home at any time," Abby stated, just as they both heard the sound of Doug's truck pulling up.

Entering the house, Doug heard Paisley's voice telling him to hurry up. He entered the kitchen where Abby and Paisley were standing.

"What's going on? Why all of the excitement?" Doug asked as he kissed Abby on the cheek.

"We have a letter from Trent!" Paisley squealed.

Abby opened the large manilla envelope to find several smaller envelopes; each addressed to each person. There was a fourth envelope addressed as "photos." They each grabbed their own personal letter and took time to read each letter to themselves. They'd each blurt out loud something to each other.

"He says his ministry is going great," Abby said.

"Trent said the food is awful," Paisley added as she giggled.

"He said he met a girl," Doug announced.

"What?" Abby and Paisley asked simultaneously.

Mary walked out of the front door with Winston and Brucy to go check their mailbox. It wasn't a long walk but long enough down the driveway to give her some much-needed exercise. Mary told her doctor that she found herself getting winded after a few small household chores. Her doctor suggested short daily walks to build her strength. Checking the mailbox became one of those walks.

She discovered three small manilla envelopes from Trent. One for Jandra, one for Neil, and one for Meemaw. Mary smiled as she gathered the envelopes and other mail and placed them in the bag that she brought to carry all of the mail back to the house. The first couple of trips gathering the mail, Mary tried to carry it all without a bag and dropped everything. It didn't take her long to realize she needed an extra hand. For Mary, a bag would suffice.

"Mail call!" Mary hollered out as she laid everything on the kitchen table.

"What are you hollering about?" Jandra asked her mom as she walked into the kitchen.

"I said mail call," she said smiling.

"Okay, is that something new?" Jandra asked as she looked through the mail.

"Only when it's exciting mail," Mary explained as she handed Jandra her envelope from Trent.

"Trent wrote! How exciting! We should get pictures this time," Jandra smiled big and immediately opened her envelope.

Both women sat down and began reading their letters, viewing the photos Trent had sent to each one. Trent knew they would all need their own photos to feel special, so he made copies for everyone. A set for his parents and a set for Paisley, a set for Meemaw, a set for Neil, and a set for Jandra. Trent even sent a letter and photos to Trista and her family. This way, no one would feel left out.

"Look at the church buildings and ruins," Jandra said in awe.

"Look at the people," Mary said with tears in her eyes.

Neil walked in and saw the two women oohing and aahing over pictures.

"What's going on?" he asked them.

"Here," Mary handed Neil his envelope from Trent.

Seeing the return address, he simply replied, "Oh."

CHAPTER SEVEN

Trent was reflecting on his return from his trip to the post office *two weeks prior*. He recalled that evening. Vince had touched base with pastors Rick and Jo and delivered any mail Amari had picked up for Pastor Jo. Business as usual. But Trent was welcomed back with disturbing news. Trent had gone into his hut and let his roommates know of his return.

"You made it back just as we're going to bed," Dylan said.

"How did it go there?" Bret asked.

Changing his clothes and climbing into his own bed, Trent said, "Fine. How did it go here?"

"Dude, some weird things happened. We'll tell you in the morning," Dylan said.

"Tell me now, what kind of weird things?" Trent inquired.

"We don't really know; it was something with that other camp," Dylan tried to clarify.

"The other camp? There is no other camp," Trent said, confused.

"It was the area where the other ministry team lives," Bret explained.

"It was where your girlfriend lives," Dylan finally elaborated.

"Binta? Did something happen to Binta?" Trent was obviously interested in knowing.

"Dude, we don't know. We'll tell you in the morning," Dylan tried to defuse Trent's curiosity.

"Tell me now!" Trent was getting loud and irritated.

"Okay, okay," Dylan realized they would have to tell him something, or they'd never go to sleep.

"All we know is that a group of guys invaded that little village," Bret stated.

"What do you mean a group of guys? Our age?" Trent needed to understand.

"Older men, guys our age," Dylan was still vague.

"What do you mean invaded the village?" Trent asked for clarity.

"Listen, Trent," Bret said calmly, "All we know is there was some sort of disturbance, and Pastor Rick told us all to stay inside our camp area. Pastor Jo said they were Tigrayans, but they shouldn't bother us. Ask the pastors tomorrow, that's all we know."

"Okay," Trent conceded. The three boys all collectively went to bed for the night. But Trent didn't fall asleep for a couple of hours. He laid in bed concerned and prayed.

"Father in heaven, I don't know what's going on, but you do. Please keep Binta safe. Please help me find answers tomorrow. Most of all, please help me not to be angry at these two knuckleheads. They have no idea what they're doing to me," Trent said, then drifted off to sleep until a rooster crowing woke him up at the crack of dawn.

Once Trent woke up and got dressed to go outside, his only agenda was to locate pastors Rick and Jo to gather information. He recalled his anxiety level and how he frantically searched for them. Trent rushed into the cafeteria tent where their meals were prepared and located both pastors sipping their morning coffee.

"Pastor Rick, what happened while I was away?" Trent walked up to the two pastors firing questions.

"Slow down, Trent," Pastor Rick said calmly.

"I can't slow down. Dylan and Bret told me something happened in the other camp," Trent said quickly without inhaling for air.

"Stay calm, Trent. I'll explain things to you. But first, tell us how your trip was and welcome the new day the Lord has blessed us with properly," Pastor Jo said with a smile.

"What? The trip was fine. I can't stay calm until I get some answers," Trent said nervously.

"Son, it is wise to greet each new morning with thanksgiving to our Lord first. Allowing fear, frustration, and rudeness is not the way to begin. Do you trust God?" Pastor Jo asked Trent.

Calming down and realizing he was acting foolishly, he looked at both pastors.

"I apologize for my behavior. I don't know what came over me," Trent confessed humbly.

"I'll ask you again, do you trust God?" Pastor Jo repeated himself.

"Yes, I do. Of course, I do," Trent said, feeling a little embarrassed.

"Then do not worry," Pastor Jo said, then sipped his coffee.

Trent wasn't sure of his next move. He wanted answers but felt he shouldn't ask. He sat down quietly at the picnic table across from the two men. He silently prayed and asked the Lord for wisdom. Trent was struggling with his instruction to remain calm. He sat still with his eyes closed.

"Trent, I understand your concern. I needed you to quiet yourself so you could hear clearly. Are your ears open now?" Pastor Jo asked.

"Yes, sir," Trent answered. He understood the difference between listening, speaking, and acting first. He recalled his parents reacting and hurting Albert instead of hearing God in their situation.

"Your friend, Binta, has an estranged uncle. Her mother's brother. He came to claim Binta as his only living relative. He and two other men grabbed Binta and two of her friends and tied their wrists to an adjoining rope that forced them to follow the three men. That is customary for this Tigrayan group. It is an old custom. The men would enslave young women. They are known as the indigenous ethnic group. But not many follow old customs. Binta's uncle is searching for financial gain or female slaves," Pastor Jo explained the best he could to help Trent understand.

"Do you mean he's looking for a payoff?" Trent asked genuinely.

"Ethiopia is a starving country. People do unthinkable things to try and ensure they will eat," Pastor Jo explained.

"Can we get Binta and her friends back? Isn't kidnapping illegal here?" Trent desperately asked.

"Unfortunately, this happens often in this country, and we are just visitors here," Pastor Jo clarified.

Trent didn't stay for breakfast but excused himself so he could go for a walk. He wasn't fully satisfied with Pastor Jo's explanation. Trent found himself walking into Binta's village. He would search for the older woman who seemed to care for Binta. Seeing the woman carrying a basket of clothes, Trent ran up to her and simply spoke as he lifted both hands and shrugged his shoulders as if asking a question, "Binta?"

The elderly woman stopped and responded in poor English.

"Taken by uncle," she said.

"Where?" Trent asked, hoping she could understand him.

"Small village up road," she pointed in a direction on the footpath.

"Okay," was all Trent could say.

"Father is white man, Alexander," she stated, then shrugged her shoulders.

"Thank you, Asante," Trent said, using both English and Swahili language to honor the woman.

Trent hadn't been able to think of anything else for the past two weeks. Tomorrow was a new day. Trent was reminded and determined to wake up rejoicing and thanking the Lord. He did trust God, and he did believe God brought Binta into his life for a reason. An overwhelming peace and happiness engulfed him. Trent knew God was speaking to his heart.

"He who finds a wife finds a good thing and finds favor from the Lord," a whispered knowing flooded Trent's heart.

"That's it!" Trent sat up in bed and yelled, realizing God just answered the true question of *What's a Binta?*

"Dude, are you okay?" came the awoken, drowsy voice of Dylan.

"Tomorrow I'm going to find my good thing!" Trent said cheerfully, then closed his eyes and rested his head on his pillow, smiling big in the darkness.

Mary continued to read Trent's letter in the privacy of her bedroom, leaving Neil and Jandra alone in the kitchen. Winston and Brucy came in from the backyard using the doggy door Neil installed years ago. Both Neil and Jandra laughed when Goliath entered behind the two dogs swatting at Winston's tail.

"That cat is something funny. He's always picking on the dogs," Neil said, making light conversation.

"Goliath is a character," Jandra replied.

Neil continued to read Trent's letter then laid it on the kitchen table.

"Trent says he met a girl," Neil said with a slight grin.

"He mentioned that very briefly. Does he elaborate and give you details?" Jandra asked, knowing Neil and Trent had a special relationship.

"A few," was Neil's short response.

Jandra felt a little awkward but decided to attack the elephant in the room.

"Neil, I have to admit something to you," she said out loud before she talked herself out of it.

"Okay," he said.

"This is hard for me because I have never experienced this," Jandra confessed.

"Experienced what?" Neil asked.

"I think it's jealousy," she finally admitted.

"Okay, what are you jealous of?" he gently asked.

"Debbie Johnson," Jandra stated.

"Debbie? Why on earth would you be jealous of her?" he questioned.

"I'm not really jealous of her per se, I was jealous that you took her out on a date," she exhaled loudly as she finally said what bothered her.

"It wasn't a date," Neil said.

"Taking a woman out to dinner is a date," Jandra informed Neil.

"Oh. Then apparently you and I have been dating for years," he said with a Cheshire cat grin.

"We take each other out often, but we also include other people. It's part of our friendship. Taking a single woman out to dinner, paying for it, and who knows what else afterwards is a date," she stated.

"What if I didn't pay?" he challenged.

"Did she pay?" Jandra asked sarcastically.

"We each paid for our own meal," Neil elaborated.

"You took her out Dutch?" she asked.

"Not on purpose," he said.

"What does that mean?" Jandra said curiously.

"It means Debbie asked me out to dinner expecting me to pay. She drank more than what the meal cost. Alcohol is expensive. A drink is fine. But you know how I feel about excessive drinking. Debbie drank so much she acted very," Neil paused to choose his words carefully.

"She acted like what? A floozy?" Jandra smiled.

"Let's just say if I wasn't a true Christian man with godly morals, she would have been an easy, tempting target," Neil admitted.

"Debbi Johnson? I know she's very attractive, seems extremely sweet, and has the tendency to over-touch men she's talking to, but," Jandra paused, also considering her word description.

"But what?" Neil asked.

"Nothing. I don't want to say something I'll have to repent for, especially when I know it's something I would have to repent for," she said cautiously.

"I'll admit she was alluring, but I'm not a hormonal eighteen-year-old boy anymore," Neil stated matter-of-factly.

"Okay, well, the issue isn't you or Debbie, it's me being uncomfortable," Jandra refocused the conversation.

"Why do you think that was or is?" Neil asked.

"I don't know. I guess I always thought of you as *my* friend, and I didn't want to share you," she said.

"Listen, I wondered why I even agreed to go out with her, especially because I kept thinking about how it must make you feel," Neil said honestly.

"Really?" Jandra asked.

"I don't know what it all means, but you're a part of my everyday life. You're my family, and your family is my family. I'm seeking the Lord about it because I'm confused," Neil confessed.

"What's so confusing? You and Jandra are a couple in everyone's eyes. Everyone but you two. If Wagner were here, he'd call it like he sees it," Mary entered the kitchen after hearing the last two sentences of their conversation.

"Wow, Mom, don't hold back. Tell us how you really feel," Jandra teased.

"I feel you're a couple. A couple of what is still to be determined," Mary kissed them both on the tops of their heads then started to make some tea.

"You're a wise woman, Mary," Neil stated.

Just then, Goliath ran into the kitchen with Winston on his heels. Goliath stopped, turned around, and jumped towards Winston with his two front paws reaching out like he was a little monster wanting to dance.

Jandra laughed and said, "Goliath, just made me realize something. Being jealous made me feel like I was dancing with a demon, and I don't want to dance that dance ever again."

"Well, it's said that jealousy is a green-eyed monster. That's why it's called being jaded," Mary chimed in.

"Right. Neil, I'm sorry if I acted closed off to you. I missed talking to you like we do," Jandra admitted.

"I missed you too. But I think we have much more to discuss. Do you want to go to lunch?" Neil asked, noticing the time.

"Sure. Is it a date?" Jandra smiled.

CHAPTER EIGHT

It was a warm morning when Trent woke up. He immediately got out of bed and dropped to his knees. Not caring about anything else, Trent reached his hands toward heaven and smiled.

"Lord, You are so gracious to me. Thank You for waking me up on this brand-new day. Forgive me for worrying about the things of this world. I trust You, and I praise Your Holy Name. Holy Spirit, I invite You into my day. Keep me focused on obeying God's Word. Thank You. I believe You touched my heart last night with instructions to find my good thing. Prepare Binta for me, protect her, and may I find favor in Your sight. Guide me in the way I should go, and I will follow. In Jesus's name, I pray, amen," Trent prayed out loud.

Dylan and Bret were awoken by Trent's voice. They didn't say anything to Trent, they both just got up out of bed, and the three of them collectively dressed to start their day.

"Dude, what were you talking about last night?" Dylan asked Trent.

"I had an epiphany," Trent said as the three of them entered the cafeteria tent.

"It's cool if you don't want to tell me," Dylan remarked.

"Okay. Hey, Bret, do you still have that Ethiopian law book?" Trent inquired.

"Sure, I didn't return it to Pastor Jo yet. What do you need it for?" Bret asked as they were seated at a picnic bench and table.

"I want to look up family laws," Trent explained.

"Alright. I'll get you the book after breakfast," Bret said.

With that discussed, the three young men ate breakfast. Trent was considering talking to Pastor Jo and Pastor Rick and sharing what he believed God put on his heart. But Pastor Rick made an announcement that they were all going on another mission hike to another village just about two miles further from St. Mary of Zion Christian Church.

Trent was excited about the mission hike. He loved ministering to the people about Jesus. He just wished Binta and her ministry team would be going. He enjoyed seeing her when their teams joined together on larger missions.

They had a few minutes to gather their Bibles, phones for photos, and any other ministry tools they used. Trent made sure his backpack had everything, including two bottles of water. He was about to go outside when Bret handed him some stapled papers in a folder called family law Ethiopia. He wanted to dive into those papers but knew ministry came first. He thanked Bret then both boys proceeded to their meeting place. He put the folder into his backpack then whispered a prayer asking the Lord to help him legally.

Pastor Rick instructed each designated team to walk together. Veronica came running up to Trent's side. Trent smiled at her and started laughing when he saw Ruby trying to catch up to Dylan.

"Dylan, slow down so Ruby can catch up with you," Trent said loudly.

"Dude," was all Dylan said as he slowed down.

"I'm glad you're my partner," Trent said to Veronica.

"Thanks, Trent. I'm glad to be partnered with you, too," Veronica said confidently.

They all walked over an hour until they passed St. Mary of Zion Christian Church.

"We should be there within half an hour if we continue at this pace," Trent said.

"Right," Veronica said as she sipped her water.

"Did you hear about the ruckus in the nearby ministry team's village?" Trent asked, making small talk.

"Yes, I did. I was actually near there talking to Liya, one of the girls who lives there," Veronica said.

"Really? Did you see anything?" Trent asked hopeful.

"A little bit. We hid behind a tent when we heard the noise," she explained.

"Did you see the men?" Trent asked.

"I saw three men and three girls pulled by a rope. I think one of the girls was your friend. The man that yelled at her was older," she said.

"What was he yelling?" Trent asked, hoping she remembered or at least heard.

"She was saying something I couldn't hear, and the man kept yelling, *Zimi Beli*!" Veronica answered.

"I wonder what that means," Trent thought out loud.

"I asked Liya, and she said it means to be quiet," Veronica answered his thought.

"So basically, the man told her to shut up?" Trent said with a smile.

"Pretty much," Veronica said.

They walked the rest of the way in silence. Trent was grateful for Veronica's candor. As they rounded a corner, Pastor Jo told the group they were close to the village. He explained these people were talked to a year ago, and just a handful accepted Christ. He shared how they were very stubborn and liked to argue. He reminded the group to stick to what they know and focus on loving these people.

"Some people respond to kindness. These people need to be treated kindly, lovingly. Anything to break their stubborn barriers. A smile speaks volumes," Pastor Jo said encouragingly.

The team nodded in the affirmative to convey they understood. About five minutes later, they saw the village. The group entered and slowly spread out in different directions. Trent and Veronica headed toward a small group of four women.

"Tadias!" hollered Veronica smiling.

"Hello," an older woman responded.

"English?" Trent asked her.

"Some," the woman answered.

"We want to tell you about Jesus Christ," Trent said.

The four women said nothing. They all just stared. Trent smiled at them as he opened his backpack to gather his Bible and tracts. A picture of Binta fell out of Trent's Bible where he kept it next to Deuteronomy 31:6 to remind him to pray for her strength and courage and to remind himself that God is with her and won't fail her.

"Hawaogopi!" another woman yelled and pointed.

"What? What does that mean? Have you seen her?" Trent asked excitedly.

The older woman grabbed the photo and said, "She is here. Hawaogopi means she is fearless," the woman said.

Trent looked at Veronica both with wide eyes and opened mouths.

"Trent, you go find Pastor Jo. I'll stay here and finish talking to these ladies," Veronica said hurriedly.

Trent put on his backpack and began running in the direction he saw Pastor Jo walking towards. He began hollering, "Pastor Jo! Pastor Jo!"

Pastor Jo walked out from underneath an awning.

"What's the matter, Trent? Why are you screaming?" Pastor Jo asked immediately.

"She's here somewhere," Trent answered out of breath.

"Who's here?" Pastor Jo asked, concerned.

"Binta."

Neil and Jandra continued their talking outside on her garden bench into the late hours of the night. They both came to the realization that they were, in fact, more than *just friends*; they were kindred spirits. They both loved the Lord, they were both born-again believers, but most of all, they were also man and woman.

Jandra had a hard time with the jealousy issue. She knew several people who had fallen victim to that lying spirit. She knew nothing good came out of being jealous, and she had never been a jealous person. It wasn't like God's righteous jealousy for His people. He is a sinless, Holy God who doesn't want His children to be deceived by Satan's temptation and lie of idolatry. God knows His plan and purpose for us. His Holy jealousy is His desire to love us and for us to know His love. Idolatry takes us away from Him. His jealousy is righteous, and we don't really understand it. Satan's always trying to imitate God, but in an evil, deceptive way. Our earthly knowledge of jealousy is nothing like God's jealousy. His jealousy is pure. Worldly jealousy tries to control another person. God's does not. Ours hurts, even kills. God's does not. God is jealous when something tries to harm us, His children. Ours is a form of sin that God wants to keep us from.

Jandra knew that her being jealous of another person was sinful and an attempt to be controlling of another human being. She knew she had no right to be in charge of another's free will. She couldn't help but remember what the Bible and the wall plaque Trista gave her one Christmas says. It read,

> Love suffers long and is kind; Love does not envy; love does not parade itself, is not puffed up; does not behave rudely, does not seek its own, is not provoked, thinks no evil; does not rejoice in iniquity, but rejoices in the truth; bears all things, believes all things, hopes all things, endures all things. Love never fails.
>
> 1 Corinthians 13:4–8a

Jandra felt ashamed. She had allowed hurt feelings to override love and her knowledge and strength to pray for all parties involved. Debbie Johnson doesn't need to be looked down upon. She needs to be lifted up to the One who can help her.

Jandra also remembered what her neighbor taught her when training dogs. Dogs and other animals resource guard. They will growl or attack if someone or another animal tries to take or threatens something that's theirs, like bones, food, or their offspring. Jandra was acting like an animal, resource guarding Neil. He was her friend, not hers to solitarily own, control, and possess. Debbie wasn't threatening Jandra, she was a threat to Jandra's insecurity that jealousy arouses. These feelings could have been avoided had Jandra remembered who she is in Christ and that she is to love both Neil and Debbie as God's Word instructs.

Neil understood all of this and explained that he felt a lot of it was his fault. He felt safe and secure with Jandra. He enjoyed living on her property and protecting her and her family from harm. He was happy to be her personal handyman on sight. However, he didn't realize he was basically taking Jandra for granted. He was becoming a hindrance to her from moving forward in her life.

Neil also realized he was leaving himself unprotected from others' temptations by not marrying and legally making Jandra his wife, instead of just a friend. As just a friend, he was living as a single man on a single woman's property, and that wasn't wise. He knew husbands and wives *are* the best of friends, especially when they invite Jesus as the Head of their relationship. There was no family hierarchy between a single man and woman in a friendship. There are no vows or covenant in living as friends. There are no covenant wedding bands that show everyone else that they are already committed to someone in the sight of God. The rings are unspoken words to suggest leaving the person wearing a wedding ring alone. It also sends the message that the person is married and in a covenant relationship, committed to another. It warns the onlooker to move on and not fall victim to sin. It reminds the wearer of the ring that they are committed to another. God is a covenant God, and He delights in marriage.

Both Jandra and Neil agreed to pray about their relationship and trust the Lord to instruct them in the way they should go. For Jandra, it's about moving forward since her husband had passed away decades ago. For Neil, it's about making things right in his spirit, so he doesn't become lustfully tempted and fall into sin. Jandra wasn't the type of woman who caused men to lust after her physically. She was attractive, but not in the Hollywood sexy way.

But Jandra's spirit was beautiful. All who met her knew that right away. She would make any man happy to be his wife. She wasn't looking for a man, but she had commented that she wasn't opposed to one finding her. She expressed how she didn't want to grow old alone if Jesus should tarry.

Neil was a fairly attractive man. Several women thought him to be a good catch. But unfortunately, the women who showed Neil any interest were married, gold diggers, or didn't want a commitment; non-Christians who just wanted to have fun. That's why he and Jandra were such good friends. They didn't have false agendas with each other. They were open, honest, and truly enjoyed each other's company. This is why they both agreed it was necessary to pray and seek the Lord's guidance.

Neil stood up and said he was going to go to his 5th wheel and call it a night. Jandra stood up and stretched, saying she was tired but wanted to do some reading before bed.

"I had a very nice day with you today," Jandra told Neil.

"Me too. We honestly have much to pray about," he said as he walked Jandra to her back door and sat on the quad to ride home.

"We certainly do. Good night, Neil," she said softly.

"Goodnight," he replied as he started up the quad.

CHAPTER NINE

Pastor Jo found Vince and another counselor, Carrie, and asked them to follow him. Trent took them down the path where he and Veronica were ministering. They hurried to where Veronica was standing. She had briefly explained to the women what was going on. The older woman seemed to know more than the others. She spoke to Pastor Jo in her native tongue for several minutes. She seemed to answer whatever questions Pastor Jo asked her.

"She explained to me that Binta was abducted for a forced marriage. The older man who took her is her uncle claiming family rights," Pastor Jo said just as Pastor Rick walked up, having found their location.

"So, what does this mean? Binta has to marry someone by force? Are there no rights here?" Trent asked with tears forming in his eyes.

"Yes and no. Yes, there are rights, but no, as family abductions for family issues, such as marriage, are often ignored," Pastor Jo answered.

"Is there anything we can do?" Trent pleaded.

"Yes, we can first find Binta, then contact Abiy Asmud Ali, a politician and the prime minister," Pastor Jo said.

There was a little more talk exchanged between Pastor Jo and the woman. Amadi, the man they all knew originally as their bus driver, heard what was being said and walked next to Trent and put his arm around him.

"Listen, the woman is explaining to Pastor Jo where Binta is. We will go there, but we have to approach calmly. You can't run in crazy, or they'll hurt you. Do you understand?" Amadi asked sincerely.

"Yes. Calmly," Trent answered. Trent ruffled through his backpack, looking for water. He saw the folder with the Ethiopian laws. He grabbed his water bottle, took a drink, then put it back. He pulled out the folder and started looking at the Table of Contents. He found Family Law on page twenty-seven. He quickly scrolled through the pages until he found it and started reading.

"Listen up, everyone. We will be walking about a quarter of a mile up this path, looking for a good size hut. It has two large pots in the front and one small tree. On the outside is a Tigray flag, which is red and yellow with a yellow star," Pastor Jo instructed his small group. Then continued speaking.

"We are going to remain calm and kind. We're there to tell them about Jesus, and maybe they will only see Jesus in the way we conduct ourselves. Understand?" Pastor Jo said, looking directly at Trent.

"Yes!" the group collectively said. Trent realized his past behavior made others nervous and concerned. But Trent knew the Lord had dealt with him on that issue and gave him a promise about Binta.

They thanked the women while Veronica and Carrie chose to linger behind to finish witnessing to them. The men began walking on the path. It didn't take long at all for them to notice the hut from the description the woman gave. They approached the large hut that was more likened to a small villa, and they heard a lot of loud talking. Pastor Jo and Amadi went to the front, and Pastor Rick, Vince, and Trent waited a few yards back.

A young, thin, dark man came outside. Pastor Jo and Amadi said something to him, and he went back inside. They held up their hands to motion to the others to stay where they were. A few minutes later, an older man came out with the thin man and another older man who was holding a gun of some sort strapped around one shoulder.

"Vrede," Pastor Jo said, which meant peace in Africa.

"Pēs," Amadi greeted the men with the Swahili way to say peace.

The three men looked Pastor Jo and Amadi up and down. Pastor Jo and Amadi held up their arms, showing no weapons, but also held up a Bible to show them why they were there. Pastor Jo had a parallel Bible of common African language and English. It helped the people read it in their own language when Pastor Jo showed them Scripture. The first older man looked Pastor Jo in the eyes.

"What you want?" the man said in very broken English.

"To tell you and your family the good news about Jesus Christ," Pastor Jo answered with a smile.

"Dehnahunu," the man said. Knowing he just said goodbye to them, Pastor Jo yelled out, "Binta!"

The man turned around, and the other two men drew near him. There was a noise inside the villa hut hollering out, "I'm in here!"

Trent felt a flush and tightening in his stomach when he recognized Binta's voice. He felt himself getting restless. The older man asked Pastor Jo in his language what he wanted with Binta. Pastor Jo explained they knew of the abduction and wanted all three girls back. He said they knew it was for marriage, but there were other ways to go about it.

Trent was holding the Ethiopian law papers in one hand and his translation book in the other. Finding the phrase he had been searching for, he yelled out, hoping he pronounced it correctly.

"Nataka kukuoa, Binta!" Trent yelled loudly.

Amadi understood Trent's Swahili attempt of asking Binta to marry him.

The older man asked pastor Jo who Trent was and what he was asking. Amadi overheard his question and said, "He wants to marry Binta."

"What's going on, Trent?" Pastor Rick asked him.

"I wanted to tell both you and Pastor Jo this morning that the Lord spoke to me last night concerning Binta," Trent started talking fast.

"What exactly did the Lord say to you?" Pastor Rick inquired.

"While I was praying, He brought me to the verse in Proverbs about the man who finds a wife finds a good thing and favor from Him. Well, as I was praying and asking the Lord to keep her safe, He spoke to my heart. I knew that I knew Binta is my good thing. This morning I knew I was going to find her. Then you announced we were going on this missionary hike. I got excited because I love witnessing about Jesus, but also because I knew deep inside, I was going to find her today," Trent explained.

He was talking so fast and excitedly that he didn't hear Pastor Jo yelling for him. Pastor Rick did and turned to see Pastor Jo waving them over. The remaining three men walked over to pastor Jo and Amadi. Pastor Rick quickly got Pastor Jo up to speed on what Trent had just told him.

"Tadias. Ibalalew Trent," Trent said the phrase he learned on how to greet someone and introduce himself.

"What you want Binta?" Dula, the older man who turned out to be Binta's uncle asked in very bad English grammar.

"I want to marry her. You know, make her my wife. Do you know the Lord?" Trent was so nervous he was rambling on.

Dula snapped his fingers, and the man with the gun went into the hut. Nothing was making sense to Trent. Dula just glared at him. Trent still had the folder sticking out of his backpack. He grabbed it, making the stapled law papers seen.

"I read I can marry Binta because technically her father was an American," Trent didn't know what he was talking about. He had read a few sentences that mentioned another country having family ties. Pastor Jo translated to Dula.

"American? Mzungu," Dula spat.

"What did he say?" Trent asked.

"White man," Amadi answered.

Trent thought of Rusty for the first time. He realized that prejudice was everywhere and worked both ways. He shut his eyes and yelled, "Ugh!"

The man with the gun came out, holding Binta tight by her left arm.

"Let go of me!" Binta was screaming.

"Zimi Beli!" Dula yelled at Binta.

Just then, Binta noticed Trent and his team. She looked with big eyes and then smiled. She said, "I knew you'd find me, Trent! The Lord told my heart this morning."

Pastor Rick knew right then that those two were meant to be. Her words confirmed what Trent had said. No one wanted to challenge an obvious sign from God. No one but Dula. Dula was still apprehensive, so Pastor Jo tried to explain in Dula's language that this was preordained, and no one would be able to stop God in this.

"You marry now," Dula said.

"Okay, how are we supposed to do this?" Trent said and looked at Pastor Jo.

Pastor Jo understood the marriage situation. He continued to speak to Dula in his native tongue. The two men spoke back and forth for nearly forty-five minutes. Legally it would take some time to get all of the necessary documents approved from the Ethiopian Government. But Pastor Jo understood that Dula was old school Ethiopian. He believed only in the wedding ritual as binding, not paperwork. Dula wanted the ritual of a wedding to feel justified handing over his only niece and remaining family member. Dula would also free the other two girls for a price.

Dula knew Binta was left with a large fortune due to her parents being killed. The government helped survivors of that massacre, especially if the survivors were children. The TPLF was a Tigrayan Liberation Front that the Ethiopian government knew caused much death. Tigray's TPLF threatened a mass genocide and other destruction to wipe out the Ethiopian people and their government so they could take over and rule themselves. The government basically laughs at their threats, but after earlier massacres, they remain guarded.

Dula prided himself as Tigrayan. His ploys were serious to him, but he failed in structure. He knew very little about the laws, as they have progressively changed over the years. However, Dula mainly goes rogue concerning the laws. Pastor Jo explained this to Trent and Pastor Rick.

"Can we do that guy's rituals, and then Binta and I really get married legally afterward?" Trent asked, hopeful.

"Are you sure, Trent? Don't you want to have your family around for something that serious?" Pastor Rick asked, knowing Trent's parents and grandma.

"We'll do it again for them if they need it, but I know the Lord is calling me to be with Binta. She is my partner in life. She is my helpmate that God ordained. Binta is my good thing. Yes, I'm serious," Trent said just as boldly as he could.

"Listen, Trent, Dula wants an Egutunais wedding. This is when the groom brings several herds of cattle to the bride's family and then just takes the wife home to his house," Pastor Jo explained. Pastor Jo also expressed that this was the simplest of all ceremonies.

"Right, so where do I get several herds of cattle?" Trent asked sarcastically.

"I think he just wants money," Pastor Jo said.

"I didn't bring a lot of money, but I brought a little. Ask him how much he will take," Trent said seriously. He learned that one US dollar equaled 73 birrs in Ethiopia. He was trying to do some math in his head about the currency when Pastor Jo walked up.

"Trent, this man wants 5,000 birrs and a virginity test on Binta at consummation," Pastor Jo said.

Trent did the math and realized the man wanted $108.11. Not a lot of money at all. Trent figured Dula was stupid or cheap. Trent brought a little over five hundred dollars cash with him. This was for personal spending money. The church supplied air fare and hotel rooms. They provided for any emergency expenses the team would need. But personal spending was up to each individual.

"I can pay him! I have the money in my suitcase. Tell him we'll pay," Trent said excitedly.

"Trent, I don't know if you understand. You will have to prove Binta is a virgin," Pastor Jo said.

"Can't she just tell him?" Trent asked.

"No. There are several ways to prove it, and his way is to see the sheets after you two consummate the marriage," Pastor Jo tried to explain this so Trent would understand.

"The sheets? What a sicko!" Trent said with a disfigured look on his face.

"Trent, a virgin will bleed her first time. If there's blood, then she was a virgin, and it is considered a legal marriage. Then you can take her back with you," Pastor Jo said.

"But it isn't legal in the United States or the government in Ethiopia. It's only real for Dula. If you do this, we will have to legally marry you here and amend it back home," Pastor Rick explained.

"Well then, praise the Lord my family will be able to witness my wedding after all. At least one of them," Trent smiled.

Trent and the others explained to Dula that they would return the next morning with the money and engage in the marriage ceremony. Trent hollered out to Binta that he would return in the morning to make her his wife. Pastor Rick kept thinking about Trent's family and how they were going to feel about all of this. Pastor Rick knew he would be held responsible. He silently prayed and asked the Lord to give him wisdom and peace in this situation. The Holy Spirit spoke to Pastor Rick's heart with an understanding that what God ordains, no man can stop. It was that thought that gave him peace.

They saw Veronica and Carrie leaving another hut when they called out to them. Hurrying, the two young ladies reached the five men.

"What happened?" Veronica asked, noticing Binta wasn't with them.

"You're not going to believe it," Trent said giddily.

"Believe what?" she inquired.

"It seems that I'm getting married tomorrow," Trent chuckled.

He explained most of it to Veronica, but Trent wanted to explain it to everyone when they returned to their camp village, which he did after the group had dinner. Trent and Pastor Rick both stood up and began explaining.

"You mean, you have to get married and pay a fee so the guy will release the girls?" Dylan asked his friend.

"Something like that," Trent said.

"Dude!" Dylan said in his normal, abnormal verbal pat on the back.

"This is all confusing and abrupt for many of you. I need to take some time alone with Trent and the counselors, so you all talk amongst yourselves for a while, then get ready for bed. Tomorrow is a new day. Get your rest," Pastor Rick instructed as he went into Pastor Jo's large hut where the team counselors were.

Veronica stood up and said loudly to the team, "Listen, everyone, this is an unusual situation. We need to pray for Trent and Binta. One man even brandished a gun."

"Also, there were two other girls that were taken. What will happen to them?" a young lady on the team asked.

"I don't know. I think there will be another fee. Let's pray for them too," Veronica suggested.

The team formed a circle, held hands, and prayed. Each team member prayed something from their hearts. In the meantime, Pastor Rick and Pastor Jo had a lot to say to Trent.

"Do you understand what must take place tomorrow?" Pastor Jo asked Trent.

"I believe I do. I am going to take Binta as my wife," Trent said.

"You do realize when you return, you will be in your regular hut with your roommates, and Binta will be housed in a hut with the girls until we officiate a real, legal wedding for you two," Pastor Rick said.

"That's fine. But I will ask that you hurry that along, please. Once I'm with Binta, I want to always remain with her. We will respect the laws of God and government, and obviously, Dula. I'm hoping Binta will be welcomed into the team for witnessing to others," Trent said.

"Of course, she will be welcomed. Pastor Jo will handle the necessary paperwork for this country, even obtain a visa for her to travel to America with us," Pastor Rick explained.

"This will take some time, Trent. You may have to fly home then return in a few months," Pastor Jo stated.

"No, I will stay here until Binta can join me. But we will be married legally in this country first. I will write to my family explaining my lingering here," Trent said, knowing Pastor Rick would say something about that.

The two pastors released Trent and further spoke to the counselors about how to answer the other members of the team's questions. This was not an invitation for the boys to find Ethiopian girlfriends or vice versa. This was something God Himself had brought into both Trent and Binta's hearts, for reasons only God knew.

Trent returned to his hut, and both Dylan and Bret congratulated him. Dylan just oohed and awed, while Bret took it more seriously.

"Trent, are you really prepared for what you'll be facing?" Bret asked.

"Prepared or not, I trust God in this. I can't explain to you two what God impressed on my heart last night and this morning. But I can explain it was and is real. I am supposed to marry Binta. She is supposed to return home with me. She was created as my helpmate. She is my preordained wife. I am her Boaz, and she is my Ruth," Trent said sternly, and neither boy challenged Trent.

"Dude, we need to throw you a party. I'll talk to the rest of the team in the morning," Dylan said.

"You do that while I'm laying with my wife tomorrow. I don't think I've ever been this nervous," Trent confessed.

"The Lord will help you, I'm sure," Bret so maturely spoke.

"Thanks, man, I needed to hear that. I feel like I'm having performance anxiety," Trent said, and all three boys laughed.

"Dude, you'll be fine. I know I'm not the greatest comfort to you, but one thing I know, you have the Comforter in you. I've known that since I met you when you started going to our church. You're different, and I believe God has His hand on you for something big," Dylan stated.

Both Trent and Bret never heard Dylan be so sincere and grownup about anything. Trent knew in his heart that God used Dylan to confirm His plan. Trent also knew that the Lord was growing Dylan up in Him. Unable to say anything, Trent just stood and hugged his friend. Finally, Trent spoke with a mist in his eyes and a slightly choked-up voice.

"Thanks, dude," Trent said, and all three boys smiled.

CHAPTER TEN

Neil was up early as his normal routine called for. While he was feeding the animals and preparing the dogs' food bowls, a thought came to him. He knew Jandra would be awake soon preparing the morning coffee, and he imagined what it would be like to wake up with her in the house. Neil realized this was literally the first time he imagined that. As he noticed a buck and a doe grazing together, he felt the whisper of the Holy Spirit, "It's not good for man to be alone."

"Lord, what are You saying to me? I think I know, but You need to make it clear to me. You know me, I sometimes second guess things. I want to be absolutely sure of Your prompting," Neil spoke out loud.

Finishing preparations for the dog food bowls and adding nuts to the higher food stand, Neil proceeded to walk towards the house's back door. Winston and Brucy came running out through the large doggy door, and Neil watched them run toward their bowls. He also looked up and caught a glimpse of the buck licking the doe on the nose.

"Now that's sweet, I should've gotten a picture of that," Neil said out loud.

"Why?" the thought of God asking him flooded his mind.

"To show Jandra, she loves stuff like that," Neil heard himself saying.

"That was for you to see because I love you," the thought of a conversation between him and God continued.

"Thank you," Neil said before turning the knob on the back door to enter.

"Thank you for what?" Jandra said as she opened the back door and overheard Neil.

"I was thanking the Lord for allowing me to see a buck lick a doe's nose," Neil said quickly, half startled.

"Cute! It was probably the buck I saw outside of my window this morning frolicking with a doe. They were like teenagers in love," Jandra said as she walked toward the kitchen table with coffee poured into two cups.

"Right. It was cute," Neil chuckled and sipped his coffee.

The two sat down and made small talk while eating donuts Jandra set out on a plate.

"Where's Mary?" Neil asked.

"Good question. She's usually awake before me," Jandra stated as she stood up to go check on her mom.

Mary was still asleep in her bed, Goliath lying next to her back, curled into a ball. Jandra didn't want to wake her mother, so she quietly closed the bedroom door.

"She's still sleeping. She must've been really tired," Jandra said.

"Let her sleep," Neil said.

"I am. She was up late looking at Trent's pictures. She misses him," Jandra said.

"I miss him too. But I think he has too much on his mind these days," Neil admitted.

"What do you mean?" Jandra asked.

"I told you he met a girl," Neil began.

"Binta," Jandra said.

"It seems he more than just met her. Trent's fallen in love," Neil said, smiling.

"Love? That soon?" Jandra questioned.

"That soon? He's not like us who takes years to know if he loves someone or not," Neil blurted.

"Right. I mean, what?" Jandra caught the comparison.

"Let's face it, we love each other. We're just slow in admitting it," Neil said as he stood up.

"Well, um, perhaps you're," Jandra began stuttering, then Neil walked over and lowered his lips onto hers. The soft kisses grew more passionately as they wrapped their arms around each other.

"Well, that was surprising," Jandra said after catching her breath.

"I guess it was. I asked the Lord to give me clarity and, in a buck-and-doe kind of way, I suppose He did," Neil said.

"Okay, I don't really get it, but when the Lord speaks, it's never up to everyone's understanding, it's only for the one who asked Him," Jandra tried to say wisely.

"I asked Him to make me sure of His promptings. I felt prompted to kiss you, and now I'm sure," Neil tried to sound just as wise.

"Okay, Mr. Sheppard, as long as you're sure," Jandra teased.

"Actually, Ms. McLain, I've never been surer of anything," Neil said and gave Jandra a soft kiss.

Mary walked into the kitchen nearly twenty minutes later. Jandra noticed her mother was holding her head and walking slower than usual.

"Mom, are you okay?" Jandra asked, concerned.

"Sit down, Mary. Can we get you anything?" Neil politely asked.

"No. I'm feeling a little ill. I'm having a bout of vertigo," Mary stated.

"I noticed you slept in later than usual. Should I call your doctor?" Jandra asked as she gave her mother some orange juice.

"I don't think so. Let me wake up more and have a piece of toast. If I don't feel any better after that, then you can call my doctor. I'm sure I'm just tired," Mary said.

"Well, I'm going to get dressed in the event that I need to take you somewhere," Jandra stated and went toward her bedroom.

"What were you two talking about?" Mary asked Neil.

"Just about a buck and doe we both saw this morning," Neil said half honestly.

"Wagner and I saw a buck and a doe cuddling up to each other the day he proposed to me. Wagner said it was God's way of telling him I'm his doe," Mary smiled at the memory.

"I think God still uses deer," Neil winked, then stood to get the bread out for Mary's toast.

Doug was vacuuming his car in the garage when his phone started ringing. He didn't hear his phone ring at first, but when he was finished vacuuming, he noticed a voice mail alert. He dialed his code to listen and put the phone up to his ear.

"I'm glad you have the same number. This is Rus Arnold. I can't get a hold of Trent, but you'll do. I'm not well, and I sort of read a little paper booklet Trent gave me years ago. I don't know what it means, but I want to know if God is real. Okay, you can call me," came the direst voice. Hurrying into the house, Doug found Abby and told her to listen. He played the message using his speakerphone so they could listen together. Abby just stared with a bewildered look.

"What do you think?" Doug asked her.

"I think he desperately needs Jesus," she said, then tightened her lips.

"I'll call him," Doug said, then used his phone's ability to call the last person who called.

"Hello?" answered Rus.

"Hello Rus, it's Doug. You called?" Doug didn't know how to start this awkward conversation.

"Yes, I did. Sorry, I didn't know who else to call. I know Trent is gone and probably doesn't want to talk to me anyway," Rus coughed as he said that.

"What can I do for you?" Doug asked.

"Trent tells me about God and that I need to talk to Him. Look, Doug, I'm alone, real sick, and I don't know what to say. I felt like Trent would want me to ask someone. I don't know anyone to ask," Rus said, depressed.

"You did the right thing by reaching out. Has Trent told you about Jesus?" Doug asked.

"I guess. I always told Trent Jesus Christ was just a cuss word to me," Rus said.

"Well, Rus, Jesus Christ is not a cuss word; He's someone who died for those who speak cuss words. He is the living Son of God who died for your sins. He took your place in the court of heaven, so to speak," Doug stated.

"I don't know all of that, I guess I need Trent to do his praying or something over me so I can die right," Rus said confusingly.

That was a profound statement, even if Rus didn't know what he was saying. Doug closed his eyes, praying for wisdom.

"Rus, no one can pray you into heaven. You have to believe in Jesus and Him crucified and resurrected. You have to accept

Him into your heart, into your life. You have to do that. No one can do it for you," Doug explained.

"Look, man, this is weird. I'm not sure why I called," Rus said, sounding defeated.

"Why did you call?" Doug asked nicely.

"I don't know," Rus answered.

"I do. Because Trent planted seeds of truth, and your spirit is hungry for that truth to be watered so it can grow. You may be sick, but a seed planted began to spring forth. Your spirit is longing for truth and life. You need those seeds watered Rus; do you understand?" Doug explained.

"Help me, man, I don't know what to do. I just don't know what to do." The voice of Rus faded then disappeared.

"Rus! Rus, are you there? Rusty, can you hear me?" Doug frantically yelled out until he heard the dial tone of a hung-up phone.

Abby asked Doug what happened when he called Rusty. Doug told her, then realized this old man needed help. Not physical help but spiritual help. Doug started dialing his phone.

"Who are you calling?" Abby asked. The phone on the other end answered, and Doug held up his pointer finger and started talking before he could answer Abby.

"Yes, hello. I would like to purchase two one-way tickets to Phoenix, Arizona," he said.

"What are you doing?" Abby asked.

Doug moved the phone away from his mouth then said, "We're going to introduce old man Rusty to Jesus before it's too late."

It was nearly evening when Abby and Doug brought Paisley over to Jandra's. Their flight was leaving in a few hours, and they wanted to have dinner with Jandra, Mary, and Neil. They picked up some pizza before arriving.

"Thanks for keeping an eye on Paisley while we go to Arizona," Abby said to her mother.

"Of course, it's our pleasure," Jandra responded.

"I'm old enough to take care of myself," Paisley interrupted.

"Of course, you think you are, but we need you here with us," Jandra answered Paisley's comment.

"Why?" she snapped as she rolled her eyes.

"Because you're too much like your mother at that age, and we can't get to you fast enough if there should be an emergency. Besides, Meemaw and I need your help around here. We're not as young and energetic as we used to be," Jandra said, then grinned big, closing her eyes blinking hard.

"Whatever," Paisley shrugged.

"Paisley, we talked about attitude," Doug said firmly.

"So, explain the big rush to Arizona. Where will you be staying, and for how long?" Jandra shifted the conversation, and Paisley bent down to pet Goliath then pet both dogs.

"Well, Doug made the hurried arrangements. We have one-way tickets, so return date is unknown," Abby tightened her lips.

"Rus Arnold called stating he has questions about God. He is very ill, apparently, and when I tried talking to him, he hung up. I believe in my heart that the old guy is in dire straits and needs Jesus. He was trying to understand some tracts that Trent had shared with him. All I know is if he dies without meeting Jesus, I will let Trent down and, ultimately, Rus. It may only take us an hour, then we'll get another flight back. Or, it could take us a week to get through to Rus," Doug explained.

"Knowing Rus Arnold, it could take a month or longer," Abby stated.

"That's okay. Just call and keep us posted. Paisley will be fine here," Jandra said as she walked Doug and Abby out to their car.

"Are you sure you don't want me to drive you to the airport?" Neil asked as he grabbed Paisley's large suitcase from their car.

"No, we'll park it at the airport. Just keep an eye on our girl and the house," Doug said as he shook hands with Neil. Jandra and Neil waved goodbye then went back into the house.

"Here's your suitcase, Paisley," Neil said as he brought it into the living room.

"Thanks. Am I in the guest room?" Paisley asked Jandra.

"Yes. Let me know if you need anything," Jandra said helpfully.

"Thanks, Grandma. You know I'm not mad at you. I'm just mad that my parents run to help that Rusty guy when all he has been is mean to them and rude to Trent. I don't understand why they rushed to get on a plane," Paisley admitted.

"I think it's because your dad has a sensitive heart when it comes to unbelievers. He wants them all saved," Jandra smiled and left Paisley to herself in the guest room and returned back to the kitchen where Mary and Neil were.

"I see a lot of Abby in that girl," Mary said.

"So do I. I just need to have silent, gentle understanding," Jandra said.

"What does that mean?" Mary asked.

"I'm not real sure, but it's what the Lord whispered to me about how to handle Trista and Abby years ago. I'm thinking I should strive to treat Paisley the same," Jandra sighed.

"It's a brilliant thought. I will consider its full meaning when I pray tonight. Lately, the Lord has put it on my heart to look at old family photos and pray over the people in them," Mary admitted.

"Is that what you're doing in your room at night?" Jandra asked.

"Yes, sometimes. It started when I received the photos from Trent. I have a strong feeling Trent needs prayer coverage. I don't know why, but it's just a feeling in my heart that Trent covets our prayers," Mary told Jandra and Neil.

"Maybe he'll write us again soon. I'm sure he's fine and desiring to return home in less than three months. I can't wait to see him and hear all about his trip," Jandra said.

"Knowing Trent, he's making the best of his journey," said Neil, smiling.

CHAPTER ELEVEN

It was an early fall morning in Ethiopia. Trent awoke earlier than the others to read his Bible, hoping for some encouraging Scripture. He wasn't nervous about informally committing to Binta, but he was nervous about his family being upset when he told them the news of his staying longer than five months and the reason why.

Trent felt compelled to read the first chapter of Joshua, but his eyes landed on Deuteronomy 31:8, and he kept reading that over and over and then out loud. "And the Lord, He *is* the One who goes before you. He will be with you; He will not leave you nor forsake you; do not fear nor be dismayed." Then he turned to Joshua 1:9 and read out loud. "Have I not commanded you? Be strong and of good courage; do not be afraid, nor dismayed, for the Lord your God is with you wherever you go." He closed his eyes and opened them to see Dylan and Bret waking up.

"Morning, Trent. Are you ready to face today?" Bret asked.

"Like my grandpa Wagner used to say, I'm ready's brother *been* ready," Trent smiled.

The two boys chuckled, causing Dylan to become fully awake. Before anyone could say anything else, Trent stood up to get dressed. Putting on his Levi jeans, he looked at both boys and said, "Hey guys, I'm going to ask pastors Rick and Jo if you two and Veronica can come with us today. You both can be my groom's men and Veronica a witness."

"Cool! We'd love that," Dylan said.

"Thanks for thinking of us," Bret stated.

"Why Veronica?" Dylan questioned.

"Because she knows the whole situation and has been very helpful to me. I don't want to exclude her," Trent said humbly.

They were all three ready and grabbed their backpacks to go out, so Trent quickly grabbed his money and took his cell phone off of the charger. He wanted someone to take pictures for his family and his own keepsake.

Trent spoke to the pastors about allowing Veronica, Bret, and Dylan to attend. Pastor Jo said it would be fine. Veronica was so thrilled that she would be a part of this. She ran back to her hut to grab her backpack, and then they waited for Amadi to arrive before they left to retrieve Binta.

Trent silently talked with the Lord in his spirit. He thought within himself, *We are retrieving Binta, I am receiving her. Your gift to me.* Trent felt the peace of the Holy Spirit flood him. He smiled.

"Dude, are you smiling about your marrying Binta?" Dylan asked as respectfully as he could.

"Something like that," Trent answered.

The seven of them walked down the trail. Pastor Rick assigned all of the counselors to pray for them and to do a small Bible study on ministering to the lost. Pastor Rick wanted to keep everyone focused on why they were really there in a foreign country.

Arriving at Dula's hut, Pastor Jo told everyone to wait while he let Dula know they were there. Pastor Jo went to the front opening, and the older man with his gun came outside. They spoke briefly then Pastor Jo waved for everyone to come into the villa-looking hut.

They entered to find it quite large, considering it was actually a hut. There were four separate areas that Trent assumed were like bedrooms. Dula came out wearing a flowing white, yellow and red robe that covered his entire body. He started talking and spoke back and forth using his native language and his broken English. The thin, dark-skinned man they had met the day before came out into the area of this large room. He motioned for Trent to stand on the left side of Dula while he placed the others in a half-circle row around them. He led Veronica to the far right, where an elderly woman who exited one of the rooms came out and stood. It was evident the women and men were to stand separated.

Once everything was to Dula's approval, he snapped for the older man with the gun to bring Binta out. She came through what looked like a burlap curtain wearing a yellow gauze-looking dress. All Trent could see was how beautiful Binta was to him. Her eyes found Trent's eyes, and they both smiled at the sight of each other. Carefully, Bret took a photo of the people and Trent and Binta seeing each other. Pastor Jo obtained permission for Bret to take some photos. He was allowed to take six total. One had to be of the wedding sheet stained with virgin blood. That alone would be Dula's wedding license, so to speak. Dula would keep the sheet, and Trent would have the picture.

The awkward ceremony was quick. Dula said words that Amadi translated to Trent, and in his broken English, Dula said, "Binta marry only if virgin and you take if she virgin and you pay wedding price."

Trent understood. The older man with the gun grabbed Trent's right arm, then walked him over to where Binta stood, then got between the two as he grabbed Binta's left arm. There was nothing gentle about the man's demeanor. His gun, now strapped across his side, kept hitting Trent's arm as they walked. Trent imagined what would happen if he grabbed the man's gun and turned the tables on things. But Trent wasn't the violent type, so his imagination faded. Basically, the man just escorted Trent and Binta into one of the makeshift rooms and thrusted them into it.

The older woman followed and entered in behind them, carrying a clean white sheet. She laid it on a mattress that was on the floor. She said something in her native language, and Binta nodded yes. Then she left Trent and Binta alone.

For the first time in weeks, Trent hugged Binta and kissed her. Binta began to remove her dress.

"What are you doing?" Trent asked, startled.

"Trent, we must consummate the marriage then we prove I am, or was, a virgin. That's why the sheet. Didn't anyone explain it to you?" Binta asked.

"Well, yes, but it all seems so rushed," Trent explained.

"Unfortunately, it is because my uncle Dula is totally naïve, and this is the only way he'll let me go. I'm still not sure about my friends who are tied to logs in another room. If we don't do this, he'll not consider us married and will keep me for another man he can receive payment from. I know this is an unorthodox way, Trent, but I love you and believe this is of God for you and me to marry. Please, let's consummate," Binta said with a longing in her eyes.

"Binta, I know the Lord would have us marry. We will only do this for Dula's sake, but we will marry legally in the sight of God and witnesses later. Today we consummate, soon we will forever make love as husband and wife," Trent said and held Binta's face as he kissed her. He helped her remove her dress, and she helped him remove his clothes. Naked, they laid on the mattress and consummated the marriage.

When they were finished, they both got dressed. One final kiss, then Trent pulled the burlap curtain to the side of his face and peaked out. Being spotted and waved on by the older woman, Trent went out to where the men were. The older woman grabbed the sheet and brought it and Binta out to join them. Dula opened the wadded-up sheet to inspect it in front of everyone. Seeing blood caused by her virginity, he grabbed Binta's hand and placed it in Trent's. Then Dula said loudly in Swahili, "Kumalizika!"

Pastor Rick asked Amadi what Dula said. Amadi said, "He said it has ended. It's finished."

Trent handed the $110.00 in US currency over to Dula.

"I know I went a little over, but you can keep the change," Trent said with a sarcastic smile, then grabbed Binta's hand and exited the hut. His wedding party of three was in tow closely behind them.

Pastors Rick and Jo were discussing the release of the other two girls with Dula. Outside, Trent's friends were congratulating the two, and Bret was making sure he took six allowed pictures. Bret was called back in to show Dula the photos he took and was released once the wedding sheet photo was clearly seen. Dula nodded and told Pastor Jo that makes it legal. He said Binta was free to go, but the other two must stay until more payment could be decided. Bret left when he heard the men loudly discussing the two girls.

"I guess it's done, except that payment for the other girls is being discussed. Now let's take a picture of you two while we're allowed," Bret said as he snapped a few photos of Trent and Binta smiling at each other and kissing.

Pastor Jo reminded Dula that legally he could no longer hold the two girls. They were not his kin, and it would be considered kidnapping. Pastor Jo gracefully explained that he didn't want to get the authorities involved, but he would if Dula didn't release them. It took another hour, but Dula finally released the two girls. They ran outside to Binta, crying.

"We're so sorry we couldn't help you," one said tearfully.

"Don't be sorry, God has blessed me. I have a family now, real family," she kissed Trent on the cheek when she said that.

Trent held Binta's hand, squeezing it, and said, "Now Pastor Jo will do the necessary paperwork for us to legally marry here in Ethiopia, then get you a visa. Binta, soon we'll be going home to America."

Trent knew he couldn't say when, but he knew God had His perfect timing.

Landing in Arizona around midnight, Abby rested her head on Doug's shoulder before he got up to retrieve their carry-ons.

"Are you okay?" Doug asked.

"Yes. I'm sure this is just where we need to be. Trent will be happy we came here," Abby said.

"Yes, he will be. We'll have something to write to him about, besides how much we miss him," Doug added.

"I wonder what he's doing. Do you think he misses us as much as we miss him?" Abby sighed.

"Of course. We're his family. It's not like he has another family there," Doug said.

"He has a spiritual family with him," Abby reminded Doug.

"You're right. But it's not like family, family," Doug said as he grabbed the one large suitcase Abby packed with both of their clothes. The carry-ons had each one's necessities, and they each carried their own.

"I guess you're right. A little less than three months, and he'll be home," Abby smiled as they opened the doors to their rental car.

"Let's find a Holiday Inn and call it a night," Abby said, tired from their late-night flight.

"You got it!" Doug smiled.

As they were driving, Abby thought about her son. She wondered if Trent was lonely. She thought about him being in a strange country all alone. For the first time, Abby heard a quiet whisper in her heart, *Trent's never alone, I'm with him.*

CHAPTER TWELVE

Jandra was pleasantly surprised when she woke up to snow falling. That's one thing she could depend on at Diamond Lake; snow. It was mid-December, and Christmas was only a week away. Trent would be arriving home in a little over a month. Jandra was so excited. He had written a couple of letters, mainly to send photos. Jandra felt it was time to hear from him again.

Hearing Neil ride up on the quad, Jandra hurried into the kitchen to pour him a cup of coffee. Much to her dismay, she saw that no coffee had been made. Usually, Mary awoke first and prepared the coffee. Jandra leaned back to look at Mary's bedroom door and noticed it was still closed.

"Good morning," Neil said as he entered Jandra's kitchen through the back door.

"Good morning. Coffee will be ready in a few," Jandra replied.

"Where's Mary?" Neil asked.

"Good question. She's probably still asleep. She's been sleeping in longer lately," Jandra said, looking at the clock.

"She's obviously tired," Neil answered and smiled.

Pouring Neil and herself a cup of coffee, Jandra sat down at the kitchen table.

"I can't stop thinking about Trent," Jandra confessed.

"I'm sure he's fine. There's probably a lot to do there," Neil said, easing Jandra's concern.

She and Neil sat gazing into each other's eyes as they sipped their coffee. Neil was about to say something when the phone rang and interrupted the moment.

"Hello?" Jandra answered, picking up the receiver.

Neil watched the color drain from Jandra's face.

"Where is she now?" she replied to the voice on the other end of the phone.

There was a long pause. Jandra hung up the phone as tears welled in her eyes.

"What happened? Who was that?" Neil stood up as he asked.

"That was someone who lives about a mile away. My mom was walking, aimlessly, disoriented, and the woman's husband picked my mom up and drove her to his house, where she is now. The woman said my mom was cold and making no sense, but she finally said my name," Jandra said as she grabbed a jacket and her car keys.

"Let me drive," Neil said, grabbing the car keys from Jandra.

"Okay, she's a mile up the road at the big yellow house with the huge wrought iron fence," Jandra explained as they got into her SUV.

They drove the five minutes in silence. Arriving at the house, Neil and Jandra rushed to the front door. Immediately, a heavy-set woman in her bathrobe opened the door.

"Jandra?" she said, opening the door wide for both Neil and Jandra to enter. She led them into the kitchen, where Mary was sitting, sipping tea. "She's in here," the woman announced.

"Mom! What are you doing here?" Jandra asked, very confused.

"I don't know, honey, I think I'm at the wrong house," Mary answered, then stood up.

"Okay, Mom, we'll take you home now," Jandra said as she helped Mary to the front door.

Neil thanked the couple for taking care of Mary and calling Jandra.

"I've seen this before, with my own mother," the elderly man said.

Jandra smiled, then asked, "What did you do?"

"I prayed a lot. But it doesn't really matter what I did. You have to think about how you're going to handle this." The man grinned then closed his front door.

"That was kind of abrupt," Jandra stated.

"That's the least of your concerns. What time does Mary's doctor come in?" Neil asked gently as a way to redirect Jandra's focus.

"I think around nine. I'll call soon and see if I can make an emergency appointment with her," Jandra said as she exhaled a heavy sigh.

"What's wrong, dear?" Mary asked.

"Nothing's wrong? Mom, where were you going this morning?" Jandra asked.

"I was looking for Goliath," Mary answered.

"Goliath is at home, Mom. It's cold and snowing, and you don't even have a jacket on," Jandra stated as she turned the heater on full blast.

Pulling up to the house, Jandra closed her eyes as if praying.

"It'll be all right," Neil said encouragingly.

"Will it?" Jandra frowned.

"There you are!" No note, just the dogs waking me up to feed them. Where were you?" Paisley asked as she ran a brush through her tousled hair.

"Nowhere, honey. We'll talk about it later," Jandra said with a warm grin, realizing she totally forgot Paisley was there.

"It must've been nowhere. Meemaw came in looking like she just stepped out of bed," Paisley added.

"Right. Don't worry, it'll be okay," Jandra stated without realizing she just volunteered unnecessary information to a child.

"I don't know what you're talking about, but realizing I never know what's going on, I'll trust you that everything will be okay," Paisley rolled her twelve-year-old eyes and left the room.

"It will be all right," Neil said, squeezing Jandra's shoulders.

"Will it?" Jandra sighed.

Doug and Abby were rested up and ready to seek out Rusty. They knew this day would be challenging, but they were determined to reach this man. They drove to the last place they knew Rusty lived. It was a small one-bedroom house in a run-down neighborhood. It had boarded-up windows and had weeds about two feet tall.

"Look at the place," Abby said, shocked.

"It's obvious Rus hasn't lived here for some time. I'm surprised it's even standing," Doug said as he pulled into the driveway.

"I'm surprised he didn't sell it. But then again, who would want to buy it?" Abby said sarcastically.

Doug got out and peered through a window that wasn't boarded. He said there was nothing in there. A middle-aged woman from next door came over and walked up to Doug.

"Can I help you?" she asked as the lit cigarette she was smoking dangled from her bottom lip.

"Do you know Rus Arnold?" Doug asked her.

"Who wants to know?" she asked with a hideous snarling look on her face.

"I'm looking for Rus. Do you know where he is?" Doug asked kindly.

"Why would I tell you?" the lady barked.

"Look, we don't want any trouble. We're just trying to locate the whereabouts of Rus," Doug said, then headed toward his car.

"Are you a friend or foe?" she asked loudly as Doug was opening the car door.

"Something like that," Doug answered, not really answering the woman.

"Just ignore her, Doug, we'll go to the police station and ask," Abby yelled out.

"Police station? What did ol' Rusty do?" the woman asked.

"Nothing, we're just looking for him to give him some news," Doug responded as he sat in the driver's seat.

"What kind of news?" the woman continued her line of questioning.

"Let's go, Doug, this woman seems strung out on drugs," Abby blurted.

"Listen, honey, you better watch your manners. Rusty doesn't want to be found," she said as bait to keep Doug talking.

"We have a message from Trent, but you probably don't have a clue who that is," Doug said.

"Trent? We all know about Trent. Why didn't you say so?" the woman backtracked her venom.

Doug seemed to be getting irritated with the woman's nonsense. He shut the car door and started the engine. She ran up to Doug's car window and knocked on it.

"He's at the rehab center. He had a stroke or something. That was months ago," the woman stated.

"Okay, thanks," Doug said boyishly and waved goodbye to her.

"Why do you encourage people like that?" Abby asked.

"I don't know," Doug laughed as he sped away.

"Where to now?" Abby asked.

"To the only rehab center I know of out here. If Rusty's there, we'll find him." With that said, Doug programmed his navigator to find the quickest route.

"I hope he's there," Abby said.

"I hope he's alive," Doug said.

Trent heard a strange noise then looked at his watch. It was the middle of the night. He laid in bed, trying to figure out what that noise was. Then he heard it again. It sounded like someone was walking into things. He knew everyone in their village was still asleep. Maybe it was a wild animal getting into things. He closed his eyes then heard the loud noise getting closer and closer. It sounded like someone was banging two metal pots together. It was loud. Loud enough to wake Bret and Dylan up.

"Dude, what's that noise?" Dylan asked, yawning.

"I don't know," Trent replied.

"Should we go see what it is?" Bret asked as he got out of bed.

"I don't know," Trent answered.

"Should I grab a flashlight?" Bret asked suggestively.

"I don't know," Trent said.

"What do you know? Dude, are you awake?" Dylan asked Trent frustratingly.

"I don't know. I mean, I don't know what we should do, if anything," Trent rambled, hoping to hide his uneasiness.

The crashing metal sounds came again. This time, all three boys were awake and alert and grabbed anything that they could use for protection.

"I'm sure everyone heard that noise. Let's grab our flashlights and check things out," Bret said boldly.

"Okay," Dylan and Trent agreed.

The three young men carefully left their hut and walked towards the direction the noise was coming from. Pastor Jo came out with a lit lantern, and Amadi was behind him, carrying a club of some sort. The loud clanging sound erupted the silence again. There in the shadows were two young men carrying two metal pots, each hitting them together, making the noise.

"You there, what do you think you're doing?" Pastor Jo yelled out as Amadi snuck behind one young man and bear-hugged him, causing him to drop his pots.

"Let go of me!" the taller man said to Amadi.

"We are here to rescue Binta, she is betrothed to me," the shorter, younger man claimed.

"Where are you from?" Pastor Jo asked the two young men.

"We're from the next village over. Binta is from our village," the taller man said as Amadi loosened his grip on him.

Pastor Rick came out just in time to see Trent, Dylan, and Bret walk up. He wanted to get to them before Trent heard Binta's name being talked about. But Pastor Rick was too late.

"What did you say about Binta?" Trent hollered out.

"She is betrothed to me to become my wife," said the short young man whom they later learned was named Leor.

"You're lying. She married me," Trent said firmly as he walked closer to Pastor Jo.

"Not so. I was promised Binta a long time ago," Leor said, pursing his lips.

"By who? Her uncle held our ceremony last week," Trent found himself defending his status.

"Hey, aren't you from that missionary team?" Dylan interrupted.

"We are missionaries, yes," Leor answered Dylan.

"Okay, boys, there seems to be a misunderstanding here and confusion which ought not to be. It is very late, or early, depending on your sleeping habits. Tomorrow you come back, and we will resolve this. If you are a servant of the Lord, then you know your behavior tonight was ghastly. There will be consequences. Do you both understand me?" Pastor Jo said authoritatively.

"Yes, sir. We will be back," Leor said agreeably, and the two left without their pots.

"What was that all about?" Trent asked.

"Don't fret. Everyone goes back to their hut. We still have about four sleeping hours," Pastor Jo declared.

In their hut, Trent, Dylan, and Bret discussed what had just transpired. They were awake, and their adrenaline was flowing.

"Dude, those guys were from Binta's missionary village. I saw them when we teamed up together about two months ago," Dylan stated.

"He's crazy if he thinks he can come here and claim Binta while waking the whole village up," Bret added.

"Too bad Binta didn't come out. She could've busted his bubble," Dylan said, snickering.

"The hut she's staying in is clear across our village. Didn't you notice no girls came out? Those guys only disturbed our side," Trent said seriously.

"Pastor Jo will resolve this in the morning," Bret said, then added, "You know Trent, you have had your patience tested a lot. I wonder if the Lord is preparing you for something huge where you'll have to have patience like never before?"

"I hope not, but if He is preparing me, I pray I will pass the test," Trent said as he laid back on his cot, closing his eyes. It only took minutes until all three boys slowly fell back to sleep.

CHAPTER THIRTEEN

Early evening Jandra sat in her living room alone with her hands against her forehead as she leaned forward. She couldn't help hearing the words of her mom's doctor running through her mind. Early-onset dementia. A list of symptoms to watch out for was given to Jandra. There were only the confusion and memory loss of the day that she could recall.

Paisley walked into the room and sat in one of the recliners. She stared at Jandra for a few moments in silence before she spoke.

"Okay, Grandma, I'm ready to hear what you have to say. Please don't say I'm too young, because even if I don't totally understand, I will understand what I need to know," Paisley said wisely.

"You're right. Well, it seems Meemaw has the onset of what's called dementia. It means she's confused and forgets things a lot. It's nothing to be afraid of; we just have to become aware of her fragility," Jandra began to explain.

"I understand that. My teacher in school shared with the class about her mom's dementia. It actually became a spelling word we had to use in a sentence with explanation," Paisley stated.

"Okay, then you know what we're up against. That darn confusing spirit," Jandra said, smiling.

"Grandma, I think it scares you. Meemaw is your mom. I would be scared if something happened to my mom," Paisley admitted.

"Well, God did not give us a spirit of fear. So, I will trust Him to walk with me through this valley," Jandra confessed.

"Don't tell my mom until you have to. She gets worried over everything," Paisley said, defending Abby.

"Okay, I won't," Jandra said as she hugged her granddaughter. Then added, "When did you get so smart?"

"I've been smart. You grown-ups just don't know how to accept that," Paisley smiled.

"Accept what? I hear you two talking," Mary said, entering the living room.

"Mom, you're awake from your nap," Jandra stated the obvious.

"Yes. I need to tell you that I don't believe what the doctor said about me. I am perfectly fine and coherent. I simply slept walked, and woke up somewhere else. I'm sorry if it caused you to worry," Mary announced firmly.

"Mom, I knew you were okay. It was a rare thing. I'm not worried," Jandra spoke as if to a five-year-old.

"Don't patronize me either. Let me say this, if something is attacking my mind, then I pray Jesus takes me home before I get to be a burden," she rebutted.

"Mom, you'll never be a burden. I wasn't talking about that anyway," Jandra tried to refocus the conversation.

"Besides, the Lord and I have a deal. If I get too old in my mind, I want Him to take me home to Him and Wagner immediately. I miss your daddy so much. Do you miss him, Jan?" Mary was rambling like a young schoolgirl. Jandra's heart was breaking for her mom.

"Yes, Mom, I miss daddy very much. I can't wait to see him, too," Jandra got up and kissed her mom on top of her head.

Jandra went into the kitchen to start dinner. She would make Mary's favorite dish. Baked chicken, mashed potatoes, and cheesy toast. She pulled out the pan and the thawed chicken. Laying eight pieces on the pan she began seasoning them. In the midst of sprinkling some seasoning salt, Jandra broke down. She sat on a kitchen chair, lifting her head up.

"Lord Jesus, I need You. Mom needs You. I am a little frightened. I'm losing it!" she cried.

"Trust Me, you're not alone," a voice in her inner heart whispered.

Neil opened the back door and walked in. Jandra smiled.

Abby and Doug made it to the North Mountain Medical and Rehab Center in Phoenix. Doug had gone there to visit an ex-coworker of his when they lived near there in Arizona several years ago. It was the first one that came to his mind, so he was praying this was the one Rusty was in. Together they walked to the reception desk. The young lady working there saw them approaching.

"May I help you?" she said, friendly and smiling.

"Hi there. We're looking for Rus Arnold?" Doug said confidently.

Looking on her computer screen and typing in the name, she said, "Oh yes, room 209. That's on the second floor. The elevator is down that hall to your left," she said, pointing. She handed each of them visitor passes to wear clipped onto their outer garments.

"Thank you," they both said simultaneously.

Finding the elevator, they pressed the going up button.

"I can't believe he's actually here," Abby said as they entered the elevator.

"My coworker, Dan, was here for a month after his knee surgery. It's the only place I knew of," Doug admitted.

"The Lord showed us favor here," Abby admitted and prided herself for giving God the credit. It was a new exercise Dr. Rhonda suggested she start doing, giving God the glory in all things He does for her.

It was only three rooms down from the elevator. They both walked up and entered cautiously. They saw Rus lying on his bed watching the television set located on the wall facing him.

"Hello there, Rus, guess who?" Doug announced softly as not to disturb the roommate behind the closed curtain in the middle of the room.

"What? Oh," Rus said in a raspy voice.

"Hello, Rusty," Abby said with a half-smile.

"How are you feeling?" Doug asked.

"My legs hurt, and I'm still alive," Rusty said in his ridiculous greeting.

"You're still using that old line?" Abby reprimanded.

"It's all I know," Rusty responded.

"I guess you're wondering why we're here," Doug jumped right in.

"The thought crossed my mind. You're a long way from Oregon," he coughed and spat in a tissue.

"Well, Rus, you called us, and we felt it was our duty to come straight to you and deliver the answers you were looking for," Doug explained.

"Oh yeah? What am I looking for?" Rus asked sarcastically.

"I believe you're looking for peace," Doug stated.

"And you're going to give me that?" Rus asked.

"Not us, but Jesus Christ can," Doug said matter-of-factly.

"You sound like Trent. Is that boy still in Africa?" he sighed loudly.

"Yes, he is. But we're not here to talk about Trent. We're here to talk about your need for salvation," Doug said.

"How do you know I need salvation? How do you know I'm not already saved?" Rus challenged Doug.

"He's not!" a voice from the next bed hollered out from behind the separation curtain.

"No one asked you, Pedro," Rus hollered out in response.

Abby looked around the curtain and smiled at the man lying in the next bed.

"Why did you call him Pedro? Is that his name?" Doug asked.

"I don't know. It doesn't matter. All of those brown-skinned fellows are all the same," Rust spat vehemently.

"Do you even know what Pedro means? It means Peter. A strong rock, like what Jesus called His disciple. You're not saying anything negative. You're actually complimenting him," Doug stated with a tight grin.

"What do you want? To see me sick in this place?" Rus said, changing the subject, knowing he'd been beat and was embarrassed.

"We're not trying to put you down, Rusty, but it seems you're still trying to put other people down," Abby chimed in.

"What do you know?" Rus responded.

"I know you've acted like a prejudiced fool for years. Maybe what I want is to see you changed. Maybe what I want is what Trent wants," she said, irritated.

"And what is that?" Rus asked with an angry frown on his face.

"You need Jesus!" Abby said loudly and walked out of the room.

"Amen!" the voice in the next bed shouted.

"Rus, seriously, you called us looking for help to understand something. I want to help you. You must be tired of living the way you do. What's wrong with you anyway? Did you have a stroke?" Doug gently asked in a calming voice.

"I had a heart attack, and when running tests, they found stage four lung cancer," Rus admitted.

"I'm sorry to hear that," Doug said sincerely.

"Trent doesn't know, and I don't want to tell him. He'll probably think I deserve it," Rus stated sadly.

"No one deserves that. Have you prepared for the worst-case scenario?" Doug inquired.

"Yes, all of my affairs are in order," Rus admitted.

"Have you prepared to meet your Maker? Are you prepared to meet God? Because whether you believe in Him or not, you're going to meet Him," said Doug.

"I'm scared, man. No, I haven't made peace with Him," Rus said in a humble forlorn voice.

"Do you want to?" Doug asked.

"Can I?" Rus questioned like a young child.

Abby listened from outside the door. She knew Rusty was close, so she opened her small purse-size Bible to 1 Corinthians 6 and walked into the room.

"Rus, can I read you something?" Abby walked in, asking with her Bible open.

"Sure," he responded, coughing and spitting into a new tissue.

Abby read verses nine and ten that listed several ungodly behaviors that she personally knew about Rus and even herself. Then she slowly read verse eleven.

"And such were some of you. But you were washed, but you were sanctified, but you were justified in the name of the Lord Jesus and by the Spirit of God." Abby had tears in her eyes.

Doug saw the bewildered look on the face of Rus. So, he further explained what Abby had just read.

"Abby just read a list of the most dehumanizing, shameful, immoral acts that we've done and that haunt our every memory. Not only does the shed Blood of Jesus Christ forgive us completely from our sins, we are sanctified, which means we are set apart totally for Jesus. We are justified, which means God totally sees us as not guilty for what we've done. You see, Rus, salvation not only forgives our sins, but Jesus Christ brings absolute purification. But you have to believe Jesus died on the cross for you. You have to receive Him as your Lord and Savior. You've read the tracts that Trent left for you and believe them to be true. It's not enough that we believe; you have to believe and receive Him for yourself. Are you ready to meet Jesus and have your sins forgiven?"

He looked at Doug, then he looked at Abby with tears rolling down her cheeks.

"I believe I'm ready," Rus Arnold declared as he nodded affirmatively with tears streaming out of his eyes.

There was more Scripture shared, like John 3:3–16; Romans 3:21–26 and 10:3–13. Doug led Rus through a prayer for sinners, which Rus repeated after Doug. When Rus said Amen, Doug read one final verse, 2 Corinthians 5:17, "Therefore, if anyone is in Christ, he is a new creation; old things have passed away; behold, all things have become new."

"You're brand-new Rus Arnold, and you're now our brother in Christ!" Abby squealed.

"Amen! Hallelujah!" the voice behind the curtain yelled.

Just then, a nurse walked in the room and said, "What's going on here?" she smiled as she prepared to do the patients' vitals.

"I'm born again! I'm forgiven. God loves me!" Rus gleamingly told the nurse.

"Awesome! Unfortunately, visiting hours are over," she said, slightly frowning at Doug and Abby.

"One last thing. Can you take a picture of the three of us?" Doug asked the nurse.

"Of course." She held up Doug's cell phone and said, "Smile." She took two photos of Rus in the middle of Doug and Abby.

"I'll get one printed up for Trent, and I just sent a copy to your phone, Rus," Abby said as she kissed Rus on the cheek goodbye.

"We'll come back tomorrow," Doug said.

Riding down in the elevator, Abby said, "Today was a miracle. I can't wait to tell Trent."

Returning the next morning, Doug and Abby walked up to the reception desk.

"Hello, may I help you?" a new receptionist asked.

"We're here to see Rus Arnold in room 209," Doug said.

The woman typed the information into the computer. She then picked up the telephone and called someone.

"Is everything okay?" Doug asked.

"Yes, just a moment, please," she said.

It didn't take but a minute for a man in a white smock to greet them.

"Hello," he introduced himself as Rus Arnold's doctor. Doug and Abby introduced themselves.

"Is everything alright?" Abby asked him.

Looking at the clipboard he was holding, the doctor said, "Seeing that your names are on Mr. Arnold's next of kin visiting list, I regret to inform you that Mr. Arnold passed away around midnight. I'm so sorry for your loss."

"What?" Abby gasped.

"If it's any consolation, he whispered that he was going home just before he passed. He left this note on his tray." The doctor handed them the note and walked away.

Abby opened the note. It read:

Abby, Trent, and Doug. Please forgive me for everything I've done or said, and thank you! Love, your brother Rus.

"Praise God, he did go home," Abby said smiling.

"Praise God, we made it here in time," Doug said.

CHAPTER FOURTEEN

Trent awoke with a zeal in his bones. He felt his honor was in need of defense, and he was going to defend it. His first mistake was thinking this battle was his. His second mistake was thinking his strength was his. His third mistake was just thinking.

Pastor Rick came to Trent's hut and asked the three young men if they would join him in a word of prayer. All three were eager and grabbed each other's hands.

"Lord, we come in Your name, and we lift this day to You. There are some issues we all will be dealing with, and we're asking You to go before us in this battle, as we know the battle is not ours, but Yours," Pastor Rick began, and Trent felt an uneasiness stirring in him.

"Jesus, we know our strength is in you alone. So, we ask your Holy Spirit to equip us in our words and thoughts. May we steer clear from thinking we know anything except you," Pastor Rick continued until Trent interrupted.

"I'm sorry, pastor, but everything you just prayed has convicted my spirit. I was in a very prideful, self-centered frame of mind this morning, and I need to repent. I awoke ready to fight a battle that's not even mine. Please finish your prayer, but I need to ask for forgiveness. This goes beyond all I know. I pray first before everything, and I just woke up in my mind, in my own strength, which is nothing. The Lord will handle today, so please, let's go. I have nothing to offer except my faith in God," Trent confessed, then zipped up his jacket. He felt like such a hypocrite and felt ashamed. He just wanted to get this over with. Trent thought that maybe this was his test for patience, and he blew it.

They all exited the hut together, and Pastor Rick pulled Trent aside.

"Trent, it seems as if you're operating in fear which is why you depended on yourself. Fear rejects God's abilities and believes we have to do something. It becomes fear because we know we can't do anything apart from Christ. Fear denies our faith, and we become afraid and confused. My suggestion for you is to forget about your insecurities and just rely on the Lord. He really is faithful even when we are not," he said, and Trent agreed. They walked to the entrance of the dining hut and noticed Leor and his tall friend were there. Pastor Jo walked out, as did Binta and Veronica.

"Hello fellows, it seems we're all here. Since you came abruptly loud voicing your intents last night, we will ask you to speak first," Pastor Jo said, and everyone looked at Trent, expecting a response. Surprisingly, there was nothing but a silent, humble young man.

"I came last night to stake my claim on Binta as my betrothed wife. It is my understanding she was taken here by force," Leor stated.

"Leor, are you nuts? I was never betrothed to you, and my lunatic uncle and his friends kidnapped me. Trent rescued me, and we were wed. No betrothal, no nothing. You are very inappropriately out of line! I suggest you leave this village and go back to where you came from. Oh, and you may want to think of repenting before God, as you came falsely and rudely. I wonder if you ever were called by the Lord to be a missionary. The only thing you are called to is a—" Binta grilled Leor but was interrupted by Trent.

"The only thing you are guilty of is false information in your mind. I'm sorry for this reality check, but you are mistaken, my friend," Trent said empathetically.

"Binta, I'm sorry, but I thought you declared your love for me. Remember when we performed the nativity skit for the children in that little village we ministered to a few years ago? I said you are my Mary, and you agreed. I thought when I said I was your Joseph, it was clear that we were betrothed?" Leor said ignorantly with childish innocence.

"You see, there, this is a misunderstanding. Do you understand Binta is no longer a young girl in an act with you? Do you understand this was unwarranted?" Pastor Jo said humbly.

"Do you understand that we were kids, and I never said I loved you?" Binta added.

"I am sorry. Of course, I understand. But this friend of mine encouraged me differently. He flooded my thoughts with twisted lies. I am embarrassed," Leor said and glared at his friend.

"Remember everyone, the Bible says in 1 Corinthians 15:33, 'Do not be deceived: Evil company corrupts good habits.' We have witnessed what happens when we're not careful of the company we keep," Pastor Jo stated and turned this unfortunate display into a Bible lesson.

Trent walked up to Binta and gave her a hug. He knew the Lord had silenced him, especially after his egotistic attitude first thing in the morning.

"You're a feisty one," Trent whispered playfully in Binta's ear.

"And you're a quiet one," Binta whispered back.

"I made a mistake this morning, and the Lord was dealing with me," Trent whispered again.

"I'm impressed that you're so obedient," she smiled.

"I don't want to talk about this anymore. I actually feel sorry for Leor. But a great reminder to choose our friends carefully," Trent remarked.

Pastor Jo and Pastor Rick walked up to Trent and Binta and gave them some good news.

"I will be able to legally marry you both in three weeks. But Binta's visa will take about five months. You are welcome to stay here until May if you'd like, Trent. Once married, you will have your own hut. But the missionary work must continue. Do you agree?" Pastor Jo asked.

"Of course, I do. Binta's my wife. I'll never leave without her, and God's work is first on the agenda for us," Trent said smiling.

Binta was smiling back at him.

"You'll need to come with Amadi and me for the mail run next week. Pastor Jo has an office in the city where we can call your family. Then you'll be back in time for your real Ethiopian wedding that all of your friends here can attend," Pastor Rick encouraged.

"That sounds great. Thanks for all of your help," Trent said.

"Seek the Lord about preparing your parents' hearts. A wedding and five more months. That's a lot to inform them about; a lot for them to swallow," Pastor Rick said wisely.

"It sure is," Trent acknowledged.

"Will your family be happy for you?" Binta asked when they were out of others' earshot.

"My family are wonderful Christians. They'll be pleasantly happy for *us*. There's only one guy I know who is never thrilled for me. The best part is I don't owe him any explanation, and I don't even have to see the man. I'll tell you all about him once we are able to talk alone for hours because that's about how long it will take to explain Rus," Trent said warmly.

"Hours, I can't wait. There is much I'd like to share with you, too," Binta added.

Trent held Binta in his arms and thought about the things they would share. They really didn't know everything about each other. Trent couldn't wait to hear more of Binta's life. Then he thought of sharing his family with her. They would welcome Binta, he was certain. Everyone but Rusty. Then again, he didn't consider Rusty as family. Trent chalked Rusty up as a lost soul no one could reach. Rusty was the perfect setup for a miracle, but Trent didn't see that happening. Trent wondered if Rusty was his test on patience? Then Trent wondered, *why should I even care?* Trent knew, if God had something for him to endure, He would give Trent all of the grace he needed.

"I can't believe you gave up so easily," Kofi, Leor's tall friend, said.

"Gave up? Who said I gave up? I don't like the smug looks those Americans gave us. No, my friend, it's not over," Leor stated.

"What about the missionary stuff and God?" Kofi asked.

"That was for Binta's sake and that Pastor Jo. I'm no longer interested in missionary work if God doesn't hear my heart. I wanted Binta. If there's really a God, He would've given her to me," Leor said.

"I may be your scapegoat friend, but I'm not sure I want to mess with God," Kofi proclaimed.

"You believe such things?" Leor questioned.

"I'm afraid not to!" Kofi exclaimed.

Doug and Abby were able to get a late flight home. Arizona would handle all of Rusty's affairs. As for Doug and Abby, they didn't have anything to do with anything. The only thing they were responsible for now was telling Trent. They just didn't know if they should write him or wait until he got home next month.

"I can't wait until I tell my mom what happened. She knows what I went through with Rusty," Abby chuckled.

"We all went through a lot with that man. Now he beat us home to glory. Who would've thought?" Doug responded.

"Who would've thought he'd become our brother in Christ? Trent is going to be amazed!" she squealed.

"He sure is. He has worked on Rus for years," Doug added.

"I bet Trent won't have anything better to share than we do!" Abby said, glowing.

CHAPTER FIFTEEN

It's been two weeks since Mary's incident and the doctor's diagnosis of onset dementia. Jandra was thrilled that there had been no further problems. Perhaps Mary was right; it was a moment of sleepwalking. Yet Jandra never knew her mother to have a sleepwalking episode. Jandra decided she wouldn't focus on what happened that morning. She would just act normal, but she'd keep a close eye out.

"Jan, what shall we have for dinner?" Mary asked.

"Whatever you'd like," Jandra responded. Her house seemed empty now that Paisley was back home with her folks. Jandra kept thinking about the news Abby brought home concerning Rus passing away hours after giving his life to the Lord.

"Hey, Mom," Jandra sat down close to Mary, then continued, "What do you think about old Rusty?"

"I think the Lord's timing is perfect. He's never too late to bring a lost sinner into His sheepfold," she squeezed Jandra's hand.

"You're right about that. The Lord has been busy in gathering this family," Jandra said.

"What do you mean?" Mary questioned.

"Well, take Abby, for instance. Her and Trista were at odds for a while, then she and I had our problems. But the Lord brought a restoration I didn't see coming, and now Abby and Doug are married and live up here in Oregon near us. We're all together, and we've had such great bonding times together. I feel so blessed," Jandra rambled on.

"It hasn't been easy. We've suffered losses. And Trent is not here with us," Mary spoke in a humble tone.

"But he'll be home in a month, give or take a day or two," Jandra said cheerfully.

"That's true, but he wasn't here for Christmas or New Year's Day. I'm missing him so much. The Lord's doing mighty things through that boy. We miss him, but we can't rush God," Mary let out a long sigh.

Neil came walking into the living room where Jandra and Mary were sitting. He kissed them both on the top of their heads.

"I'm so glad you two stopped playing games with each other. We don't have time on this earth to be coy," Mary stated.

"Who is being coy?" Jandra laughed.

"At least when I go home, I'll have something to tell Wagner. You know he has a lot to say about relationships," Mary's eyes glazed over as she smiled into the air. Neil and Jandra looked at each other.

"Is she okay?" Neil asked Jandra.

"I think so. I really don't know," Jandra was saying as the phone rang.

"Saved by the bell," she said as she picked up the receiver.

"Hello?" Jandra said as she answered the phone.

It took a few seconds before she understood through the staticky connection.

"Trent!" Jandra screamed. Bringing Mary back to reality and Neil's face lighting up. She put the phone on speaker so they could hear too.

"Hi, Grandma!" Trent said happily.

"Neil and Meemaw are here too. You're on speakerphone," Jandra said bubbly.

"Hey buddy, how's it going?" Neil said.

"Well, it's going good. It's almost 5:00 a.m. tomorrow your time. I'm at a hotel with Pastor Rick on the monthly mail run. I'm sending more pictures to you all," Trent said.

"Hi, honey, I'm so glad to hear your voice," Mary said.

"Hi, Meemaw, I'm glad to hear your voice. I miss you all," Trent said.

"Did you talk to your mom?" Jandra asked. She didn't want to say anything about Rusty if he hadn't talked to Doug and Abby. It was their story to tell.

"I'm calling them next. I wanted to call you all first before I talked to them," Trent said, easing into his news, sort of paving the way for his folks.

"Thank you, you know we're happy about that, but your mom probably needs to hear your voice! She has news to tell you," Jandra said nonchalantly.

"I have news too. Are you all sitting down?" Trent asked.

"Yes, we are. Talk to us," Jandra's eyes got big with excitement.

"My trip is going to last another six months," Trent blurted, then closed his eyes, waiting for their response.

"Ministry going that well?" Neil asked as he shrugged his shoulders as Jandra glared at him.

"It is, but I'm getting married in a week, and Binta won't be able to obtain a visa for at least five months," Trent announced boldly without hesitation. There was silence for a few seconds.

"Congratulations!" Neil was the first to say something and break the ice.

"That's great, Trent, but why the rush?" Jandra asked.

Trent gave them the entire story in five minutes. They all sat in disbelief. They had so many questions but kept in mind that the ministry was paying for this long-distance call. Long-distance was an understatement; it was an overseas call and probably very expensive.

"It's complicated, but I really love Binta. This was definitely of God, I assure you," Trent explained.

"I don't doubt that at all. I've always known the Lord had a special plan for you. Six months is a long time, Trent. But no matter what, I want you to know I absolutely love you, and Binta is already loved by us," Mary said so brilliantly.

"Thanks, Meemaw. I hope my mom takes it as good as you all," Trent said.

"Trent, she'll be fine. I remember when you first started seeking God. I knew right away your life was not going to be ordinary. Please know we love you, and we're looking forward to more pictures and meeting Binta. We sent some Christmas pictures the other day, but I don't know how long it takes for you to get our mail," Jandra said, encouraging him by giving him something to look forward to.

"Don't lose faith, Trent. We're all praying for you," Neil said, a little choked up.

"Thanks, Neil. Thank you all. I love and miss you all so much," Trent choked up.

"We love you, too," Jandra said as she let a tear fall down her cheek.

"Oh wait, Pastor Rick is going to explain more to you while I go call Mom and Dad on a different phone," Trent said, then handed Pastor Rick the phone.

"Hello, Jandra?" Pastor Rick said.

Blinking her eyes to clear out the tears, Jandra said, "Hello Pastor, it seems you have a lot to tell us." Jandra sat down on the couch closer to Neil and held his hand, squeezing it.

Trent dialed his parent's phone number. Each ring made his stomach tighten in knots. He was grateful someone answered by the second ring.

"Hello?" came Paisley's voice.

"Hello, little sister," Trent said smiling.

"Trent! Oh my, Mom! Dad! It's Trent!" Paisley began screaming.

Abby and Doug rushed to where Paisley was standing, catching her last words to her brother.

"I miss you, too! Here's Mom and Dad. Send more pictures, I love them!" Paisley quickly handed the phone to Abby, who had her hand stretched out, while Doug put the speaker on.

"Trent, it's Mom. How are you, honey?" Abby said, choked up.

"And it's Dad, you're on speakerphone," Doug announced after Abby spoke.

They all exchanged a few pleasantries then Trent announced why he called.

"I was allowed to call because I have some news for you," Trent shared.

"We have some news, too. But you go first," Abby kindly said, practicing patience.

"Okay. Mom, don't freak out," Trent began, not realizing telling Abby not to freak out only made her freak out.

"Go ahead, Trent," Doug spoke up.

"I'm going to be staying here a little longer," Trent eased into the blow.

"How much longer?" Abby asked as she lowered herself onto a nearby chair.

"Six months," Trent blurted it out and waited for their response.

"Six months? Is your witnessing going that well?" Doug asked.

"That's funny, that's the same thing Neil asked me," said Trent.

"Great minds think alike," Doug added, without questioning why and when Trent was talking to Neil.

"Why so long? What's happened?" Abby asked as she started to sound frantic.

"I'm getting married in about a week, and it'll take Binta five months to get her visa to come home with me." There it was. Trent just gave up the announcement as if it were mere information.

"Married?" Abby and Paisley asked simultaneously.

"Yes, Mom. But the good news is I can have another wedding ceremony there in the states with you all once we're home."

"Oh, that is good news," Abby said as she started clapping her hands loudly.

"Dad, is Mom okay?" Trent asked.

"Well, Trent, I'm not going to lie. She's being sarcastic, and her face no longer has a huge grin on it," Doug stated.

"I had to marry Binta," Trent said, sounding desperate.

"Did you get that girl pregnant?" Abby scolded.

"No, of course not. Look, I love her, but her uncle put pressure on me," Trent tried to explain.

"Where's Pastor Rick? Why were you pressured? Couldn't Pastor Rick reason with her uncle?" Doug questioned without knowing any of the facts.

"No." Trent slowly tried to explain what he could to the best of his ability. Trent would rely on Pastor Rick to help clarify things to his parents.

"I don't like it. Wait until I tell your grandma," Abby said.

"I already talked to Grandma, Meemaw, and Neil. They're all understanding and happy for me," Trent said, commending himself for calling them first.

"That explains your comment about Neil," Doug said.

"Well, I think this is great news. Congratulations, Trent. Tell Binta I'm happy to have a sister-in-law," Paisley announced.

"Thank you, Paisley, for being so mature," said Trent, hoping to convict his parents.

"You're welcome. By the way, Mom and Dad have something to tell you. I'm leaving the room now so you all can talk in peace. I love you!" Paisley announced and left her mom's glare to go into her bedroom.

"Don't worry, Mom. God has His hand all over this marriage. Tell me what your news is," Trent diverted the conversation.

"Our news. It's good news. Rusty gave his life to the Lord," Abby started but found it hard to speak. She felt as if her breath was sucked out of her.

"What? How do you know?" Trent asked, amazed.

Doug began telling Trent everything, beginning with the phone call he received all the way to ending with Rusty's conversion and death. Trent was trying to process the news. Rusty was dead. He wondered if his attempts to reach him succeeded, or did his parent's attempts succeed? Trent felt a little betrayed by God that God took Rusty before Trent could ask Rusty to forgive him for quitting on him. Trent felt he was robbed of forgiving Rusty for being such a prejudice, sarcastic bully. Trent just closed his eyes. He wondered if Rusty asked for Trent's forgiveness. Thoughts were swirling in his mind.

"Are you okay, Trent?" Doug asked.

"I will be. Pastor Rick is here to explain more about my situation. I love you and miss you," Trent stated and handed the phone to Pastor Rick, who had just entered the adjoining room.

Trent nodded at Pastor Rick as he opened the hotel room door and stepped outside. Trent crouched down against the wall and began sobbing. His mind was racing. What hurt Trent's heart the most was the fact that Trent just blamed God for betraying him. Trent had never blamed God for anything, let alone for betraying him. Trent couldn't handle what he felt. It was like committing mutiny against God. He first accused God of betraying him, when in reality, Trent didn't even take the time to thank Him for Rusty's salvation.

"What is happening?" Trent cried out loud. He had just experienced a fear of turning on God and falsely accusing God of turning on him.

"Lord, I'm sorry," Trent sobbed.

"I know. I forgave you years ago when My Son stepped on the cross. I'm not surprised, but you will be if you don't stand firm and dust yourself off. You need to be ready for the things that are coming your way. You need to be confident that I am with you and will never leave you," Trent felt the Lord saying to his spirit.

Trent stood up and dusted himself off. He knew there was much more he had to process. Living in shame was not one of them. Trent went back inside the room clearing his throat. Pastor Rick was seated on a chair near the only table.

"Are you okay, Trent?" Pastor Rick asked.

"God won't let me be any other way," Trent said confidently.

"Your dad told me about Rus. Praise the Lord he received Jesus before it was too late," Pastor Rick said cheerfully.

"I think I failed Rusty and God. I think I gave up on him too early," Trent responded.

Pastor Rick knew all about Rus Arnold and Trent's relationship. Trent didn't hide anything, and he kept no secrets. Pastor Rick opened his Bible to read Scripture to Trent:

> But avoid foolish and ignorant disputes, knowing that they generate strife. And a servant of the Lord must not quarrel but be gentle to all, able to teach, patient, in humility correcting those who are in opposition, if God perhaps will grant them repentance, so that they may know the truth, and that they may come to their senses and escape the snare of the devil, having been taken captive by him to do his will.
>
> 2 Timothy 2:23–26

"You see Trent, I believe you did reach Rus. Your efforts were seeds planted that were watered in time and they were able to break the grip Satan had on Rus. God had a plan for Rus. You did your best to fulfill your part in God's plan," Pastor Rick said, hoping to encourage Trent.

Trent said, "I did everything I could for Rusty."

Pastor Rick said, "And God did everything you couldn't."

CHAPTER SIXTEEN

Trent was preparing for his wedding ceremony. He stood outside of his Ethiopian hut and was amazed that in January the weather was in the low seventies. The sun was shining a warm ray upon the fields near the little village he was staying at. He thought about his family in Oregon. Trent knew they were experiencing snow and very cold temperatures. When he shared with Binta about the weather in Oregon, she would get excited. Her father grew up in Michigan and told her stories of playing in the snow. Binta longed for that experience.

Pastor Rick had explained Trent's entire situation to his family, and though Abby was a little reluctant, she accepted Trent's decision. Trent was so excited to make Binta his wife. He looked up at the sky and wondered if this was how Christ felt as He prepares to come for His Bride—the Church.

Amadi and Bret were stepping in as Trent's bridegrooms. Binta had Veronica and Liya as her bridesmaids. Dylan was Trent's best man, and Aida, one of Binta's childhood friends that lived in her old village and was also taken by her uncle, was there as her Maid of honor.

Pastor Jo had applied for and received a legal marriage license for Trent and Binta and would officiate the ceremony himself. Pastor Rick agreed to handle everything in the United States upon their arrival. Vince would step in as their photographer while Carrie and two other counselors handled the wedding lunch preparations.

Everything was ready. Even the elderly woman from Binta's old village who took care of Binta arrived with a few others; as guests. Pastor Rick came to Trent's hut and told him it was time. The three young men walked out together and stood where Amadi was already standing, on the right side of Pastor Jo, who had on a beautiful burgundy robe that he wore on special occasions. It denoted his pastoral authority.

A young, bronze-colored boy with jet black curly hair and emerald eyes was playing the Kebero, which was a small double-headed drum wrapped in animal skin that was used in traditional Ethiopian ceremonies. The boy was quite skilled and knew his responsibility in advancing the wedding ceremony. He played a certain pattern of beats for Trent's entrance, then switched to another pattern of beats that announced the bride's arrival.

Since everyone was already standing, they simply turned toward the bride's entrance. Clearing a path so Binta and her bridesmaids could walk, the crowd whispered aloud. At one point, Binta stopped and remained standing still as her bridesmaids took their places on the left side of Pastor Jo.

As Binta stood there alone, the drumming intensified as Trent walked over and grabbed Binta's hand, leading her to Pastor Jo. Nothing was like the Telosh, a very traditional Ethiopian wedding; instead, they were instructed by Binta and her desires. Binta wore a beautiful purple scarf over a white Habesha Kemi. This was a cotton fabric made into an ankle-length dress Ethiopian women wore for special occasions.

Binta walked with her head up, shoulders back, and holding a bouquet of wild flowers made by Aida. Binta's hair was braided and pulled up, and she adorned many golden necklaces and bracelets. Carrie loaned Binta some gold and purple stud earrings to wear that accented Binta's face, causing her beautiful copper-skinned glow to radiate her beauty.

When Binta stood before Trent, he was mesmerized by how amazing she looked. She was not America's bride in a flowing white laced wedding gown; she was a young woman clothed in grace, wrapped in the arms of Jesus, prepared in strength and beauty to meet her groom. She was the most beautiful woman Trent had ever seen.

Pastor Jo led the bride and groom in the exchanging of their love affirming vows to each other and the exchanging of rings. Binta had her mother's wedding ring, made of sterling silver and genuine Ethiopian opal. She had given it to Aida to give to Trent to put on her finger during the ceremony. Pastor Rick had taken Trent to buy a nickel silver, zinc alloy Ethiopian ring when they were in the city during their mail run. Pastor Rick gave the ring to Binta to put on Trent's finger when it was time.

The ceremony was quaint, with the small group of Trent's Oregon ministry team and several of Binta's Ethiopian missionary friends as witnesses. Trent and Binta promised to love each other forever, no matter what came their way, then kissed passionately when Pastor Jo pronounced them as husband and wife. Whistling and clapping were heard, and both Trent and Binta smiled at each other and embraced longingly.

Traditionally, all of the guests were invited to dance and toast with Tej, which is an orange-colored honey and alcohol drink served at weddings. The only difference was the fact that there was only a "sip" of the drink for everyone to use as a champagne toast. There was a punch made as the beverage which they could all enjoy with lunch. Everyone was treated with lunch, and a cake was made for the finale. Vince took numerous photos using his cell phone.

At the end of the evening, Trent and Binta were given a small hut that would serve as their first home for the remaining of their time in Ethiopia. It was prepared and set up for the newlywed couple to live in. All of Trent's belongings were brought to their new hut by Dylan, as well as Aida bringing all of Binta's belongings. It was all a part of the best man and maid of honor's responsibilities.

Finally, darkness covered the warm Ethiopian sky. Trent and Binta laid down together in their newly assigned bed. Trent held Binta close to his body and whispered in her ear.

"I will take care of you, my wife, for the rest of my life," Trent said.

"I will take care of you, my husband, for the rest of my life," Binta commented back, pressing her lips against Trent's. Holding Binta close to him, Trent spoke aloud, "Sovereign God, we thank You for marrying us today. You are our amazing Father, and we will serve You, together, all of the days of our lives. You are welcome as the Head of our marriage," Trent prayed.

"No matter what the future holds, we will give You the glory," Binta added. Together they said, "Amen," and proceeded with their kissing.

A few huts over, Vince started looking at the many pictures he took. They were all very clear and included each person there in attendance. Vince smiled when he saw a photo of Bret and Veronica dancing. Vince laughed when he saw a photo of Dylan tasting the Tej and squinting his eyes together. Vince scrolled through them slowly, enjoying the day's events for a second time.

Then something caught his attention. Leor, the trouble maker, was amongst the visitors at the table where Binta's old village members sat for lunch. Vince hadn't noticed Leor before this photo. If he had actually seen him there, surely, he would've said something. Leor looked as if he was leaning down, talking to the elderly woman who helped raise Binta. This troubled Vince. Obviously, no one else saw Leor, as no one else said anything. He wasn't an invited guest. He was a wedding crasher.

"Why Leor?" Vince whispered softly. "What were you doing here today?"

Vince enlarged the photo on his screen and saw something Leor was putting in the elderly woman's hand. It looked like paper, or money, or something Vince just couldn't make out clearly. He would show Pastor Rick in the morning.

Abby was the first to wake up and considered calling Dr. Rhonda. But the thought of constantly running to her therapist every time she was troubled by something troubled her even more. Abby knew Trent would be married when he came home, and then she realized he wouldn't be home for about another six more months. This was all troubling to her. But Abby made up her mind that she wasn't going to allow this to dictate her day.

Instead, Abby got out of bed and got dressed. She would get active and start being productive. She would make a to-do list and actually *do* what she puts on it. First on the list was to pray and ask the Lord what she should put on the list. Abby scribbled the words *make a list* as number two. She started laughing as she read it back to herself.

"What's so funny?" Doug said, interrupting her thoughts.

"This," Abby continued laughing as she pushed the paper towards Doug.

"Make a list? What's this for?" Doug questioned his grinning wife.

"That's what's so funny; I don't know. I felt I needed to do something so I wouldn't feel so out of control. I thought about calling Dr. Rhonda, but then I figured this is something she'd suggest I do. So, I started doing it. Then I realized I don't know what to do after praying," Abby admitted.

"Maybe all you need to do is pray, then the Lord will flood your mind with ideas," Doug encouraged.

"That's my problem, Doug. I don't know what to pray for. I'm just numb," Abby confessed.

"I think God knows that. But tell Him anyway," Doug said as he got up to make coffee.

"Maybe I'll just go to my mom's today and visit with her and Meemaw. I'm sure they have similar feelings and hopefully ideas of how we can handle things. You know, power in numbers," Abby smiled.

"That's a good idea. I'm going to church for a meeting this morning, so I'll be out of your hair," Doug said jokingly.

"You're never in my hair. You just tousle it sometimes," she kidded back.

Abby continued getting ready for the day by first preparing breakfast and making sure Paisley was awake. She'd give her preteen daughter the choice of staying home or going to Grandma's. Much to Abby's surprise, Paisley wanted to go with her.

"Who knows, I may have ideas all of you, older people, can't think of," Paisley had said.

"It's not that we can't think of young ideas, we choose to think like grown-ups," Abby replied.

"That's scary. That's also why I'll go with you," Paisley smirked.

"Oh, you're a funny girl," Abby playfully said back.

Neil walked in Jandra's kitchen door after feeding the animals and noticed no one was making the morning coffee, so he began preparing it. Jandra walked in and saw it was Neil. She noted that it was nice seeing Neil in her house first thing in the morning.

"Good morning. I thought you were my mom," Jandra said as she hugged Neil.

"Sorry for the confusion. I didn't realize I look like Mary," Neil smiled as he kissed Jandra's cheek.

"Now that you mention it," Jandra said teasingly.

She leaned back and noticed her mother's bedroom door was closed.

"I better make sure my mom is there. After the last time, I thought she was oversleeping but found out she was gone, I'm not taking that chance by assuming," Jandra stated as she went to her mom's room.

Tapping lightly on the door, she softly said, "Mom? Are you awake?" Then Jandra opened the door. Seeing pictures lying in stacks on the floor and seeing her mom lying in bed, she slowly went to the window to open the curtains.

"Mom, rise and shine," Jandra said, just like Mary used to say to her when she'd wake Jandra up. Goliath was lying curled up next to Mary's back and meowed as Jandra spoke.

"Good morning, Goliath, looks like you two had a late-night again," Jandra said loud enough to hopefully wake her mother up.

Noticing Mary wasn't moving from the noise she was making, Jandra touched her mom on the leg to shake her awake.

"Mom, wake up now," Jandra continued to shake her. Noticing Mary wasn't breathing, and her face had a blueish color, Jandra started screaming, "Mom! Mom! Wake up! Mom!"

Neil came rushing in, "Jandra's, what's wrong?"

Crying hysterically, Jandra screamed, "Mom! No! Mom!"

Neil checked for a heartbeat and noticed Mary was cold; nothing.

"She's gone home," Neil choked and dialed 911 on his cell phone.

"No! Mom! Wake up!" Jandra collapsed onto her knees, crying.

Fifteen minutes later, the ambulance sirens were screaming as they came up Jandra's driveway. Trista and Jared heard the sirens and went outside. When they realized the ambulance was going to her grandma's, they jumped in their truck to get to Jandra's faster.

Trista barely let Jared stop the truck before she jumped out, wearing her nightgown only and barefoot, Trista ran to the opened front door screaming, "Grandma! Grandma!"

Jared caught up to Trista just in time to see Neil holding Trista back as the paramedics were tending to Mary. Jared walked in and asked what had happened.

"Mary didn't wake up this morning," Neil said softly.

"Meemaw? Where's my grandma? Grandma!" Trista hollered out.

Jandra came out quickly to her granddaughter and grabbed her. Hugging Trista tightly, the sobbing Jandra said, "Meemaw went home."

CHAPTER SEVENTEEN

The next couple of weeks proved to be a blur for Jandra. Burying Mary next to Wagner was the easiest decision she'd have to make. Holding Meemaw's funeral without Trent being there just wouldn't do. Jandra asked Doug to help her make the necessary arrangements to fly Trent back for four days. Since Pastor Rick came back with the mission team, he would help.

Pastor Rick knew how to get a hold of Pastor Jo to inform Trent of the news. He assured Jandra he would conduct the funeral service as well.

Pastor Rick also wanted to find out from Trent if Pastor Jo found out what Vince had seen in the photo of Leor and the elderly woman. Pastor Rick and the rest of the team returned before Pastor Jo could investigate. Pastor Rick was concerned about that and was evenly concerned that no one saw Leor crash the wedding ceremony. His entry there was stealth. Pastor Rick's concern for Trent and Binta was still fresh in his mind. Pastor Rick was very glad and confident that Pastor Jo was aware and would handle it.

Jandra paid for Trent's round-trip ticket and had it ready to be picked up two days before the funeral. Jandra was just upset she couldn't send one for Binta, too. That would be asking a lot of Pastor Jo to sort out in such a short time.

Jandra sat on the bedroom floor in Mary's room. Jandra also sat there the evening after Mary's death and tried to clean up the floor. Mary had made piles of photos with a note placed underneath each pile. It turned out Mary was praying for each family member and wrote out a blessing over them and a personal note. It's like Mary knew she would be leaving that night.

Jandra read them and realized each person needed to read and receive their own handwritten note. Jandra put the photos and notes collectively in large manilla envelopes, with each addressed with the individual or family's names written on the outside of it. Jandra was hoping this would be something they could share at the funeral. Everyone, but Trent, agreed, and that's only because he hadn't received his letter yet.

Trent was flying into Yangon International Airport, the closest to Diamond Lake, in the morning. Doug and Abby would pick him up. Abby was so excited to see Trent. But she was so sad that this was such a heartbreaking reason for the temporary interruption.

Jandra had fallen asleep on her mom's bed but was awoken early by Goliath. Jandra knew she needed to get up and get herself ready to see Trent in a few hours. The funeral was tomorrow, but this day would be spent privately with all of her family.

Jandra got dressed and went into the kitchen to start the coffee. She watched as Brucy and Winston made their way slowly into the kitchen. She gave each dog a hug as she kissed the top of their heads. While the coffee was making, Jandra thought she'd go feed the dogs and animals herself. She added a warm coat over her robe as she noticed the ground covered with snow.

As Jandra was feeding the dogs and putting nuts and feed out for the other critters, aimlessly, she threw a few cut-up apples out near the garden the deer usually went to. Jandra went through the motions, but that was it. She almost forgot to make sure there was water in the dog bowls and not just ice.

Jandra walked back into her kitchen and hung up her coat on the rack near the back door. Seeing the coffee was ready, Jandra poured herself some coffee in her mother's favorite cup Mary used for tea. Jandra sat down, took a sip of the hot coffee then started crying. This was Meemaw to everyone, but to Jandra, this was her *mom*. Jandra wouldn't see her mom again until Jandra went to meet her in heaven.

"Mom, say hi to daddy for me," Jandra cried as tears flowed down her cheeks.

"*What about me?*" said a small still voice in Jandra's spirit.

Abby was so glad to have Trent home. Trent was sitting alone in Abby's living room, his old living room. Trent was reading the letter Meemaw had written to him. He knew Meemaw was home with Jesus, and that made Trent smile. He knew she was happy to be there with Grandpa Wagner, too. Trent believed he would see them all one day. That was his hope.

Paisley walked out and saw her big brother sitting on the couch. She threw her arms around Trent's neck and didn't say a word.

"Good morning, little sister. How are you holding up?" Trent asked.

"I'm so much better now that you're home. I've missed you. Now I miss Meemaw," Paisley commented.

"We all do," Trent said as he hugged Paisley.

"Grandma and Neil will be here in a while. Trista and Jared will be here too, with the kids," Paisley announced.

"I'm looking forward to seeing everyone. I can't wait for you all to meet Binta," Trent smiled, feeling the loneliness of being away from his wife.

"Oh yes, married boy," Paisley grabbed Trent's hand and looked at his ring. Continuing, she said, "That's big and old looking, but cool."

"I'm glad you approve," Trent said.

Doug and Abby entered the room and joined in the conversation. They all briefly discussed Trent's next wedding there. They briefly discussed living situations. They unanimously said they couldn't wait to meet Binta. Trent showed them photos on his phone of him and Binta. He also showed some photos Vince took at their Ethiopian ceremony. Abby was so proud of her son. Trent told them all of the gory details Binta's uncle Dula put them through. Abby and Paisley cringed, but Doug pat Trent on the back.

They also told Trent about Rusty's conversion before he passed. Trent felt really good that his tracts made a difference. Abby handed Trent the note Rusty had left. Trent smiled, knowing Rusty did ask for forgiveness. That made his conversion seem all the more sincere and real to Trent. He knew there's more to discuss, but everyone who would be arriving there soon.

It wasn't long until Abby and Doug's house was crowded with family. Kids were running around, and everyone was making sure Jandra was doing okay. Neil was thrilled to see Trent, so he sat near Doug while they all three talked.

Jandra went into the kitchen to see if Abby needed help with anything. She didn't. Trista had brought over sandwiches, potato salad, and lots of chips and drinks. Trista even brought an apple pie they could all share. Trista had really stepped up like Meemaw and Jandra would. Jandra was so proud of the young woman Trista had become.

Trent walked up to Jandra and put his arms around her. Jandra hugged her beloved grandson. Trent grabbed Jandra's hand and led her to his bedroom.

"What's up, Trent?" Jandra asked, smiling.

"How are you doing, Grandma?" he asked.

"I'm doing okay. I won't lie, this is very hard on me. Meemaw was my mom," Jandra admitted.

"I know. But you and I both know Meemaw is okay, and we're all here for you," Trent said encouragingly.

"Thank you. How are you? How's Binta coping with your having to leave?" Jandra changed the subject off of her.

"She's okay. She wishes she could come. She can't wait to be here. Binta had a rough life, Grandma. She also knows you wanted her to come here, too. Thank you. That meant a lot to both of us," Trent began updating his grandma on everything. Trent showed Jandra more photos. He then showed her the photo of the bed sheet and shared how humiliating it was that they had to show Dula.

"A lot of countries use the bed sheet as proof. It's a virgin's blood that keeps her and the groom safe. That blood means she's pure. Just like Christ's blood was pure. Until our sins went upon Him on the cross. He yelled, 'It is finished' when all of our sins were there upon Him, and His blood was shed for us all. Now we have the Blood of Christ that makes us all pure. He shed His blood so we can live cleansed by His shed blood and our belief in Him. The blood has life. In Binta's and your situation, it kept you both alive, safe. It allows you a life together. The blood of Jesus gives us a life together with the Father. There's no other way to be cleansed and forgiven of our sins except through the blood of Jesus Christ. It's just interesting how powerful blood is. Especially the blood of Jesus," Jandra proclaimed.

"Dula yelled, 'It's finished' or 'It's done' in his language when he saw the blood on the sheet," Trent recalled.

"I'm telling you, there's nothing more powerful than the shedding of pure blood," Jandra sighed.

"I miss talking with you, Grandma. I miss you so much," Trent said and hugged his grandma tight.

They all talked and made plans to meet at Jandra's house in the morning. They would all drive to the church together. Jandra and Neil said their goodbyes then left to go home. While driving, Neil squeezed Jandra's hand. She looked at Neil and smiled.

"Thank you for being here. You have been my rock. You kept me steady through all of this," Jandra said.

"That was Jesus, but I'm glad He used me," Neil answered.

"You're right," Jandra said and let out a heavy sigh.

He walked Jandra to her back door. He gave Jandra a very consoling embrace. Neil gently kissed her lips then whispered, "I'm done leaving you here alone. Let's get married so I can live righteously with you. Jandra, I do love you."

"Really? I love you too, Neil. Okay, let's do it," Jandra said.

"Let me take care of it. Don't worry about anything. I'll handle it," Neil kissed her lips then started the quad to ride to his 5th wheel.

Jandra walked into her kitchen. She giggled like a little girl. She raised her head up, then smiling, she said out loud, "Lord, your timing is impeccable. Please let Mom and Dad know their prayers are answered."

It was a somber morning. Jandra dressed in a black outfit. Long black skirt, black sweater, black boots, and her long hair pulled up with black hair clips. Jandra found a pair of earrings that were black metal roses. She would wear her black fur-lined trench coat. She was the next of kin, then Abby and grandchildren were next in line as survivors. Jandra felt very heavy in her spirit. She had prayed and asked the Holy Spirit to hold her up this day. It was hard when she buried her dad, but she still had her mom then. Now she was burying the woman she loved and called mom. The woman who raised her and taught her how to be the godly woman she was now.

Neil walked in wearing a black suit and was very debonair, yet humble. That's probably what attracted Jandra to Neil when they first met many years ago. He was handsome, but his humility was most attractive. No words needed to be said. They both smiled at each other, and Neil hugged Jandra. Not an intimate hug, but a reassuring one that she wasn't alone.

Trista, Jared, and their three children walked in through the back door. All dressed in dark colors. The twins were very quiet. Ethan was wearing his black suit and was so handsome. He was the most docile yet saddened. He always had a special bond with Meemaw. The children knew Meemaw was now in heaven with Jesus and Grandpa Wagner. But Ethan took his loss very hard.

Abby, Doug, Trent, and Paisley walked into the house through the front door. Doug wore a black suit, and Abby wore a very conservative black pencil skirt. Her black cashmere sweater was a Christmas gift from Meemaw, given to her just a little over a month ago. Trent wore a black suit he would no doubt wear when he and Binta had their third wedding. Their *American wedding*, as Binta called it.

Paisley was the granddaughter that stood out. She had on a pink pencil skirt that Trista handed down to her. Her sweater was maroon and pink with a gold chain-link belt around her waist.

She had on a pair of multi-colored high-top converse tennis shoes. She was very colorful. When Paisley walked in, Jandra hugged her and laughed.

"Meemaw always said life should be celebrated, and we're celebrating her life today, right?" Paisley said.

"Yes! Yes, we are. You have it right Paisley, the rest of us are a bunch of sad sacks, aren't we?" Jandra laughed.

Everyone agreed and laughed. Paisley's young brilliance lightened the mood. The family gathered together in a circle holding hands in the living room. Trista led the family in a beautiful prayer. Then they all got into their prospective vehicles and drove to the church where church friends and old friends of the family and Mary's were.

Entering the sanctuary and being escorted to their seats in the front row, Jandra was in awe of how many people came to pay their respect. The church was filled with flowers of all sorts. Beautiful arrangements of carnations, lavender, and baby's breath were displayed around Mary's coffin.

Pastor Rick Mauer stood off to the side podium and began Mary's eulogy. He read the twenty-third Psalm and a few other verses Mary treasured. "Amazing Grace" and "How Great Thou Art" were sung by a church member in the choir. Mary always greeted the young lady and commended her on having a beautifully powerful voice. Jandra made sure this gal would sing.

There was a time afforded for anyone who wanted to share something in their hearts about Mary. Jandra was the first to go to the microphone set up opposite the podium just for speakers. Jandra carried the note Mary had written for her.

"I believe my mother, Mary Anne Wagner, knew she was going home the night she did. She made piles of pictures for each family member with a personal note. She even set apart pictures of my dad on top of her Bible. I won't read the entire note she wrote to me, but I will share a snippet, as our family may choose to do the same," Jandra paused then continued, "My mother wrote to me, she wrote,

'Jandra, you're now the matriarch of our family. I pass the torch to you to continue to keep our family placing Jesus first and to live according to God's Word. Don't worry about anything, your dad and I will be waiting with Jesus for our family's homecoming.'

That's my mom. She'll always be this family's matriarch. No one could carry that torch and title like her. She loved Jesus more than anyone, then my dad, and then our family. If my mom knew you, she loved you and prayed for you. Thank you for celebrating the life of the most precious woman I know," Jandra choked up at the end as she finished, then hurried to take her seat.

Abby was next. She started to say something but broke down crying. She went to Jandra and hugged her mother. Doug said some nice things, as well as Jared and Neil. Then Trista came forward.

"Meemaw, as most of us know her and called her, is the godliest woman I know. She always said what needed to be said. She orchestrated our family to seek God's forgiveness and the forgiveness of each other. One sentence, she wrote in her note to me, was for me to look for ways to love and forgive anyone who has or will wrong me. She also told me everyone has to answer to God for their behavior, so it's important to let people off of my personal grudge hook. She said much more, but that's something I hope to live by for the rest of my life. I have had to exercise those admonishments already. I know Meemaw lived like that. I pray I can live like my great-grandma," Trista smiled teary-eyed, passing Trent as she went to her seat.

"I almost didn't make it today. But I am grateful beyond measure that I did. Meemaw was sensitive to my calling from God. I know my grandma gets it from Meemaw and the Holy Spirit, and that, I believe, is due to Meemaw bringing my grandma up in God's Word. I was blessed to talk to Meemaw even though I was overseas in Ethiopia. I know she loved me. If you knew her, then you knew Meemaw loved whoever God brought in her path. Great example. Meemaw, I'll see you one day!" Trent pointed up and hollered.

Paisley spoke one sentence. "I'll miss Meemaw, but I will always celebrate her life," she chokingly said, then sat back down.

A few friends of Mary's got up briefly to pay their condolences to the family and honor Mary's memory. Pastor Rick was about to close in prayer when Ethan stood up and walked to the microphone. Neil, being closest, lowered the microphone to Ethan's mouth.

"Meemaw is my great-great-grandma. She's very great to me. She loves me, and I love her. We can't see her because she's with Jesus. Only her body is in that box. She loved hugging me, and I love to hug her too," Ethan stated, then walked up the three steps to get to the casket. Ethan stretched out his little arms and hugged the casket, then yelled, "Nope, she's not here! She's really with Jesus!"

No one spoke after that.

CHAPTER EIGHTEEN

After the service, all who attended were invited to share a catered lunch together and stay to fellowship with each other. Jandra went around thanking everyone for attending and celebrating Mary's life. Much to Jandra's surprise, there was Debbie Johnson.

"Hello, Debbie, thank you for coming," Jandra said politely.

"Mary was always nice to me and treated me with respect," Debbie said and smiled.

"You know, Debbie, I haven't always been that welcoming. I hope you will forgive me. Perhaps I will see you as my mother did," Jandra said, grabbing one of Debbie's hands and putting her other hand on top of it, cupping Debbie's hand in between both of hers.

"You have nothing to ask forgiveness for. If anything, I owe you an apology," Debbie grimaced.

"Why would you think that?" Jandra asked.

"Well, I'm sure you know Neil and I dated, and I should've considered how that would make you feel. I didn't, and for that, I'm sorry," Debbie stated as if this was a memorized dialogue full of sarcasm.

"Well then, you know how close Neil and I are. I knew all about the dinner *you* asked him out on and how it didn't go so well. Unfortunately, I know all about you, and I judged you. You, nor anyone else, deserves my judgment or opinion, and for that, Debbie, I am sorry and ask you to forgive me," Jandra said, then realized she was still judging Debbie and didn't really mean what she just said.

"Of course, I forgive you," Debbie said, smiling.

"Wait, I'm still judging you. I'm sorry. Look, I'll be honest, I don't feel that I'm cut out to be your girlfriend or buddy. You are an acquaintance, and I need to leave us as that. I won't judge you any longer, but I'm honest about forgiving you and hoping you will forgive me," Jandra said, feeling good about facing that jealous spirit. She actually meant what she had just said and felt a release of bitterness. Being honest freed Jandra.

"Sure," Debbie said nonchalantly.

Just then, Neil walked up giving Jandra a kiss on the cheek. "Hello, Debbie," Neil politely said.

"Sure," Debbie said again and walked away.

"Is everything alright?" Neil asked Jandra.

"It is. It really is," Jandra replied.

Jared and Trista walked over to Jandra and Neil. Trista hugged her grandma.

"Have either of you seen Trent?" Trista asked.

"He was talking with one of his friends from the mission team. He's around somewhere," Neil stated.

"Wow, Neil, you're so profound. I never thought of Trent being somewhere," Trista giggled and patted Neil's arm as she walked by.

Laughing, Jandra said to Neil, "You gotta love her."

Neil smirked, then excused himself. He needed to talk to Pastor Rick.

Jared and Trista found Trent. They walked Trent over to where Phyllis and Rodger Beady were. Trent knew Jared's parents, so he hugged Phyllis and shook hands with Rodger.

"How are you, Trent?" the couple asked.

"I'm doing well, under the circumstances," Trent answered.

"Right. We're sorry about your loss. Meemaw was an exceptional woman," Phyllis said.

"Listen, Trent, Jared told us all about your getting married. Congratulations. We understand you'll be retrieving your wife soon and bringing her back here. We'd like to make you an offer," Rodger said.

"What kind of offer?" Trent asked, confused.

"Well, Phyllis and I will be moving back east to her sister's. Her husband passed away two months ago, and she's having a hard time there alone. They didn't have any children but have a huge house. Since Phyllis is the only family she has, we were thinking about moving there with her. We've been wanting to move, but we didn't want to leave our cabin empty for Jared to fill. Trista suggested you and your wife move into our back cabin. Trista and Jared will be your landlord. It's up to you all to work out the details if you're interested," Rodger asked.

"Interested? Of course, I am! That's awesome! Thank you both so much," Trent hugged them both excitedly. Then hugged Trista and Jared.

"I can't wait to tell Binta," Trent smiled, thanking everyone again.

It was the evening of Mary's funeral, and the family gathered at Jandra's house for some private time together as a family. It was a long tiring day, but it wasn't over. Trent would be leaving tomorrow at noon and wanted to be with his family before he left.

They were all seated around the living room when the doorbell rang. Brucy and Winston started barking, and Goliath came running out and jumped on the top of the couch to see what was going on. Neil answered the door and let Pastor Rick inside.

"Pastor Rick, what's up?" Trent asked, assuming Pastor Rick was there to speak to him.

"I'm here for a private service. Family only, fairly informal," Pastor Rick stated.

"What's going on?" Jandra asked, looking around the room.

"Well, everyone, last night I asked this woman to marry me so I wouldn't have to leave her here alone anymore. I should've done this before Meemaw went home to the Lord, but I think she knew it was coming," Neil said.

"What?" Abby, Trista, and Paisley gasped.

"Is this why you had to find Pastor Rick earlier?" Jandra asked, grinning.

"Jandra, Neil asked me to get the marriage license a week ago. He wanted everyone to be here," Pastor Rick said.

"But you only asked last night? Actually, he said *let's get married*," Jandra shared and chuckled.

"Always the romantic," Trista added and giggled.

"Mom, we would've given you two a big wedding had we known," Abby said and hugged her mom.

"Listen, I actually talked with Trent yesterday and suggested we have a double ceremony when he marries Binta again. We can be more formal then, but tonight I just want to marry this woman," Neil said, and Pastor Rick took his place in front of the two.

Before Pastor Rick went through the marriage vows, he asked if anyone had any objections. The entire living room shouted in unison, "No!"

Neil displayed a black velvet box with three rings inside. An engagement ring, and matching his and hers white gold wedding bands. They exchanged vows and put on the rings.

"You may kiss your bride," Pastor Rick said.

After Neil kissed Jandra, looking at everyone, Jandra said, "Neil just didn't want to stay another night alone in that 5th wheel."

They all laughed and hugged both Neil and Jandra.

Trent was seated on the Boeing 747 yet again. He still had about four hours until he arrived at Addis Ababa airport in Ethiopia with Amadi there to pick him up. Trent closed his eyes and thought about the past few days. He saw some of his friends from the mission team and several people who knew and loved Meemaw.

Trent grinned when he thought of his grandma and Neil getting married. He also imagined how thrilled Binta would be for a double wedding ceremony and to know they have a place to live alone as a married couple. Trent felt himself getting excited to bring so much great news home to his wife.

Pastor Rick did pull Trent aside secretly to talk about Leor crashing the wedding unbeknownst to anyone.

"Pastor Jo may have resolved the Leor issue by the time you get home to Binta," Pastor Rick had said to Trent privately before he went home.

"I sure hope so. That guy is nothing but trouble. He seems to have a secret agenda," Trent told Pastor Rick.

"Just remember, nothing is hidden from the Lord. What's done in secret will be revealed," Pastor Rick said.

Trent thought about that. He hoped he wasn't walking into an ambush when he returned to the small village. Trent nibbled on a chocolate chip cookie his mom made for his trip. Abby actually made two dozen, now minus one, for his trip. Trent wanted to share them with Binta.

The plane was landing as Trent was wakening from a nap. He immediately went to the baggage claim. Trent left most of his clothes there with Binta. He did, however, bring a suitcase full of clothes that he could give to the less fortunate. Trista and Paisley even donated some old clothes for the girls. Trista sent a couple of tops and skirts for Binta. Trista was excited to have a sister-in-law.

Getting his suitcase, Trent met Amadi outside with the same old bus. Trent gave Amadi a hug and threw his suitcase inside the bus. It was just the two of them. They would pick up mail before they dove the fifteen hours back to Ambo. Inside the Best Western motel room, Trent pulled out a navy-blue hoodie sweat-jacket for Amadi. He never had a hoodie, and he was thrilled. No one ever gave Amadi anything special, so this gift meant the world to him.

After picking up the mail, the two young men traveled fifteen hours on the rough roads back to their village. As the old church bus entered the village hut area, Binta came running out to greet Trent.

"Trent, you've come home to me!" Binta ran to Trent and embraced him.

"Of course, I did. Next trip is you and I going to our real home. Wait until I tell you everything that happened," Trent was just as excited as she was to see him. He couldn't wait to talk to Binta and tell her everything.

Pastor Jo walked up and gave Trent a brotherly hug.

"There's good news I have to tell you," Pastor Jo said. "Get some rest. Tomorrow we'll talk."

"That sounds great," Trent said as he rolled his suitcase into his hut.

Trent and Binta spent the night holding each other and talking. Trent showed her the clothes Trista gave to her. The excitement in Binta's voice and on her face made up for every hour they were apart. As they dressed in the morning, Binta put on the melon color long knit skirt with the cobalt blue blouse. She felt like a movie star in these clothes. Trent watched her twirl around and marveled at how beautiful Binta was to him.

Pastor Jo approached Trent and Binta in the dining tent. Trent realized the village seemed empty without his team. Pastor Jo assured him that another team from a Texas missions church would be arriving in a week and a half.

"What's the good word, Pastor," Trent asked.

"Jesus is Risen," Pastor Jo said smiling.

"Amen to that, He is Risen indeed," Trent replied.

"Oh, you mean about the Leor situation?" Pastor Jo laughed.

"That came to my mind," Trent said with a grin.

"Well, Trent, it's like this, Leor tried to offer Jahzara money to buy Binta," Pastor Jo began.

"Who's Jahzara?" Trent asked.

"She's the elderly woman who took care of me. The woman in the photo," Binta explained.

"Oh. What do you mean buy Binta?" Trent inquired.

"He doesn't believe Dula asked for enough money. He offered Jahzara more money," Pastor Jo said.

"Of course, it wasn't a lot of money. I figured the guy was stupid and cheap. But what does Jahzara have to do with anything?" Trent looked confused.

"Jahzara arranged the whole kidnapping with Dula so she would get a cut of the money. The problem was Dula went cheap because he didn't want to put Binta through all of that with you not being able to afford an unreasonable price. Leor knew what Jahzara wanted, so he tried to bribe her, not realizing Binta was legally married to you when I officiated the wedding that day," Pastor Jo explained, and Binta just kept silent, adding a few uh-hums.

"That woman set the whole thing up?" Trent said, unable to grasp his mind around it.

"Yes," Pastor Jo answered.

"And Dula wasn't the mean bad guy after all?" Trent tried to understand.

"Oh, he was mean and a bad guy, but he wouldn't have even known about my relationship with you if it wasn't for Jahzara. But her greediness backfired on her," Binta said.

"Dula could've been worse, but he didn't care to harm Binta. He didn't care about the money, either. Jahzara had been working with Dula since Binta's parents were killed. They met when she had to take Binta in. But she never thought she would be wheeling and dealing using Binta. She had helped Dula purchase many young girls to sell as brides or slaves. But Jahzara began telling Dula what to do and how to handle his business, and that made Dula angry. The clencher was when Jahzara mentioned selling Binta and her telling Dula to ask Trent for a lot of US currency, that he got mad at Jahzara. She was trying to use Dula and his sister's daughter for her own gain," Pastor Jo elaborated.

"How much money did this old woman get?" Trent asked.

"Ten American dollars," Pastor Jo said, laughing.

"What did she ask for?" Trent wanted to know.

"Ten thousand American dollars," Pastor Jo chuckled.

"The Lord worked this out because He has a plan," Binta added.

"What about that whole virgin sheet?" Trent asked, feeling sick inside.

"That is one of their customs. Dula figured if Binta was still a virgin at her age, then she should be with you. The men he sells to prefer younger girls," Pastor Jo stated.

"Did you talk to Dula?" Trent asked.

"Yes. He was very forthcoming when I explained how the authorities would feel," Pastor Jo laughed.

"He's an idiot, and so is Jahzara," Binta said.

"Trent, leave it be. Leor's gone. He left his village humiliated. Binta confronted Jahzara and wiped the dust from her feet. She's through with those people. I will be talking to the authorities about Jahzara and Dula after you are both safe in America. Oh yeh, Binta's visa should be ready in three months," Pastor Jo grinned.

"Three months? I thought you said five," Trent smiled.

"I know somebody," Pastor Jo smiled.

"Who? Who do you know?" Trent asked.

"I know a man named Jesus," Pastor Jo pointed toward heaven and grinned from ear to ear.

CHAPTER NINETEEN

Three months actually turned into four, but the week had arrived where Trent and Binta were to fly home to America. They were finishing up their packing. Binta was deciding what to leave behind for her friends there. Trent was also deciding the same. He had made some new friends with the Texas team that came for a mission trip. He would leave items for them to donate to the different villages.

Binta showed Trent a leather journal with blank pages that she would draw in. Trent recognized it as the item Jahzara gave to Binta when he first saw her. Trent looked at the drawings Binta did. There were some of the huts, the village, and some of the people she knew there. There was one of her mother and father. Binta explained that's how she remembers them before they were killed. There was even one of Trent.

"These are beautiful. You're an amazing artist," Trent praised her.

"I don't have a cell phone to take pictures. God gave me my mind only and the gift of capturing what I see or what I remember. This is *my* photo album," Binta said.

"Oh boy, you're going to love my grandma. She's an artist, too. I should say she's going to love you," Trent smiled with pride in both women.

Shortly after that conversation with Binta, Trent decided to go for one last walk. He felt the need to be alone with the Lord. Trent wanted to thank God for everything he experienced in

Ethiopia. But he also felt like the Lord was tugging at his heart. Trent went to the St. Mary of Zion church. He sat on a piece of the old church's ruins. He climbed up on it and just sat.

He reflected back on the past couple of years and began sobbing. There had been a lot of loss in his life, and Trent felt as though he hadn't dealt with any of it. He began to pray, but it turned into a cry out to the Lord.

"Father in heaven, I feel a weight on my spirit. I haven't been seeking You as I used to. I pray when I need help, but I haven't taken the time to praise You and thank You for all You've brought me through and have blessed me with. I haven't truly grieved over losing Meemaw. But I figured it's because I know I will see her again. I can't put my finger on it, but I think there's something more You want out of me. Can I ask You what that may be?" Trent spoke out loud to God as if He was sitting right next to Trent. Which Trent believed He was.

Trent searched in the Scripture for an encouraging verse but came up empty-handed. He started wondering if there was anything undone in his life. Did God ask Trent to do something that he didn't do? Surely, he would do it now. Trent just held his Bible close to his heart, hugging it. He just needed to know what's troubling his spirit.

Trent opened his Bible out of despair and began flipping through the pages. His thumb was sitting on Mathew 6:14, and it caught his attention, "For if you forgive men their trespasses, your heavenly Father will also forgive you." Trent read it over and over. He wondered if he had unforgiveness in his heart. He didn't think so, but then a flood of thoughts consumed him.

Have you forgiven your mother? Have you forgiven Rusty? Have you forgiven Dula, Leor and Jahzara? Have you forgiven yourself?

Trent felt warm tears running down his cheeks. "No, Lord, I haven't forgiven them. My mother for bringing her past into my life and for forcing me to visit with Rusty. Rusty, who didn't know You, so he confessed his ignorance all of the time, angering me. The three here for causing me to worry, fear, and behave rudely, out of character," Trent admitted.

"Did any of them *make* you feel and act the way you did?" Trent felt the soft whisper of God in his spirit.

"No, Lord, I behaved as my flesh wanted to behave. I didn't show love. In fact, I despised my mom. Oh God, I'm so sorry. Forgive me," Trent cried.

"I already did. Have you forgiven your mother?"

Trent knew he needed to ask Abby to forgive him for holding a grudge against her for several years. He also knew he needed to forgive her for making choices he didn't like. Trent realized he was thinking that he needed to forgive his mother for having her own free will that affected him. He thought about it.

"Lord, if I forgive my mom for having her own free will, I'm actually blaming You for giving it to her," Trent said with clarity in his understanding. "That goes for everyone else. When I blame their actions, according to their own free will that You gave them, I'm ultimately blaming You for their actions. I mean, it's like I'm mad at You for giving them a free will," Trent heard what he said and fell to his knees.

"Forgive my ignorance. How is it I should feel I need to forgive You for the gift You gave to each of us? How can I blame You for being just and equal to each of Your creation? Who am I to blame You for anyone's behavior that You allowed them to choose for themselves? What's wrong with me? You're God, and I am not," Trent beat his breast.

"You're forgiven, Trent. Now show mercy on others as I have shown mercy to you," Trent heard God whisper to his spirit. Trent understood he cannot righteously hold a grudge against anyone. He felt so small, so insignificant. Trent felt ashamed for even feeling angry with people who hurt him. But Trent heard the whisper of God tell him that Christ died for his shame. He just needed to forgive others as Christ forgave him. The Lord also reminded Trent that if anyone purposely hurt him that vengeance belongs to the Lord and not to Trent. Trent felt the burden, and the weight of unforgiveness lifted off of him.

Trent stood up and dusted off his knees. He held his arms up toward heaven and screamed, "Hallelujah! I'm free! Praise You, Lord! Thank You, Jesus!" Trent knew whatever was hindering him from walking in the will and purpose of God was just broken. The chains of unforgiveness fell off of Trent. His burden was lifted.

"What are you so happy about, American boy?" the familiar voice of Leor broke Trent's alone time with the Lord.

"Leor, what are you doing here?" Trent asked.

"Did you think I would forget your sarcasm? Do you think I forget you embarrassed me? Do you think I wouldn't fight for Binta?" Leor said and pulled out a switchblade.

"Listen, Leor. I'm not going to fight you. I married Binta, and we're leaving to the United States. You'll never see us again," Trent said as he was slowly moving backwards to keep some distance between him and Leor.

"I know you think you're better than me, white man," Leor growled at Trent.

Trent quickly thought about what he believed God just spoke to him. *Be merciful.* Leor continued to berate Trent by using racist comments. Having heard it too much from Rusty, Trent snapped.

"I am no better than you! You are no better than me! If you want to stab me, go ahead! But God promised me He will judge between you and me, and He will have vengeance!" Trent screamed at the top of his lungs, getting red-faced and boldly moving towards Leor.

Just then, Kofi, Leor's tall friend, showed up looking terrified. His eyes were huge, and he went in front of Leor and screamed, "Leor, stop!"

"Get back, Kofi, I will teach this boy a lesson," Leor said, waving his knife.

"In the name of Jesus Christ, get away from me!" Trent yelled.

In a flash, Leor and Kofi fell to their knees and put their hands in front of their faces as if they saw something.

"Get up! What are you doing?" Trent asked firmly.

"He doesn't see it!" Kofi grimaced.

"See what?" Trent asked.

"I don't know. It's too bright to look at," Kofi cried, then bowed down with his face on the ground in the sand.

"What?" Trent said, looking around. He didn't see anything. He did notice Leor holding his eyes and crying. Trent walked over to him and put his hand on his shoulder. Trent didn't understand what was happening, so he said out loud, "God, help them!"

Immediately after, Trent said that both Kofi and Leor were able to see. They both stood up crying and took off running and screaming.

Trent stood there alone. He didn't know what was going on. Then he heard a silent whisper in his spirit, "I am the Lord, and vengeance is Mine."

Trent started walking toward his village. He couldn't make sense of what just transpired. Then it dawned on him, "Lord, if that was You, please forgive Kofi and Leor."

Trent slightly jogged the remaining mile back to where Binta was. He never spoke of that incident for years. But he remembered those two young men every time he prayed for prejudiced people.

All Trent wanted to do now was hold his wife. He wanted to pray with Binta about their future. He felt his spirit revive after his alone time with God. Trent believed more was to come, and he was no longer hindered from seeking it.

As Trent was getting closer, he picked up speed. Just as he was turning the last corner, he heard the Lord say to his spirit, "Teach your children these truths."

"What?" Trent said and entered his hut.

Jandra woke up to Neil's arms around her. She couldn't remember when she felt so secure. They were married. No more fear of being alone in the future. Jandra rolled over and smiled at Neil.

"Good morning," Neil said.

"Good morning to you," Jandra replied.

They both held each other for a few minutes, then got out of bed. Neil got dressed while Jandra grabbed her robe. She was headed to the kitchen to make the coffee but found it was already made. So, she poured two cups and sat down at the kitchen table. Jandra grabbed her Bible to read with her daily devotional. The devotion was about the next generation in families. She read it and the corresponding verse when Neil walked in.

"When did you get up to make the coffee?" Jandra asked.

"I didn't. I prepared it last night, then set the timer for this morning," Neil said, smiling.

"I know there's a timer. I never used it because I never knew when I was going to wake up," Jandra tried justifying her negligence.

"I thought you were going to say it was because Meemaw liked doing it," Neil said, sipping his coffee.

"That would've been better. Or I could've admitted I don't know how to set the timer," Jandra laughed, blushing.

"That's what I figured," Neil smiled back.

Jandra got up to heat breakfast burritos in the microwave. She poured orange juice and set the glasses on the table.

"I'm going to finish cleaning out the 5th wheel. If you want to help, that would be fine. I actually need it cleaned up to sell it," Neil explained his day's plans.

"Do you really want to sell it?" Jandra asked.

"We don't need it here. I figured the extra money could come in handy," Neil stated.

"I thought maybe we can it pull down here to store near the garage. I also thought maybe we could travel a little," Jandra suggested.

"We can do that. I didn't realize you'd want to travel," said Neil.

"Why not? I have a bucket list of places I've never been, and I'm sure you do, too," Jandra confessed.

"Okay, I'll tell you what, you make a list of places you want to go, and I'll do the same. If we have any matching, we'll go there first. It'll be our honeymoon," Neil suggested.

"I love that idea. Let's do it!" Jandra said excitedly. She grabbed a notebook and started on her list.

Neil laughed. "Well, since we had a whirlwind wedding, we can actually plan our honeymoon together," he commented.

"We did have a whirlwind wedding. Did we get it right? I mean, I thought we were content being friends," Jandra admitted.

"We're still friends, we just did the right thing by becoming one rather than two. Now we share everything, rather than the safe things only. Think about it, I wouldn't sleep in your house because I believed it didn't seem right in God's eyes. We wouldn't even consider making love because outside of marriage, the bed is defiled. We were the best *safe* friends there was. But truth be told, we both laid in bed alone wondering if we'd die alone or if we were keeping the other from a fulfilled life," Neil said.

"Nicely said. It's all true. I was so used to you being around that the thought of you being gone was torture, so I wouldn't think about it," Jandra said.

"We've been through so much together. I couldn't think of doing it all over again with someone else," Neil confessed.

"Me neither. You've always been like family; now you are for real!" Jandra smiled.

"Well, Mrs. Sheppard, we are for real," Neil rose up to put his dishes in the sink, first kissing Jandra on top of her head.

"Mrs. Sheppard. Oh, that reminds me, I have to change everything from my driver's license to my bank checks," she said as she rinsed the dishes and loaded the dishwasher.

"You better get busy," Neil smirked.

"I'm also helping Trista prepare the Beady's cabin for Trent. He'll be home within a week. I'm so excited," Jandra said, elated.

"I'm excited to have him home too," Neil admitted.

Trent laid in bed next to Binta, and they both discussed how awesome it was going to be living as husband and wife in America.

Binta couldn't wait to see Veronica and the others she had already met while they were in Ethiopia. Tomorrow was the morning they would take the fifteen-hour drive with Pastor Jo and Amadi. Trent gave Amadi his address and asked him to please stay in touch. He deemed Amadi a life-long friend as well as a brother in Christ.

Binta quickly rolled out of bed and ran to the bucket they used as a trashcan.

"Are you okay? What are you doing?" Trent asked, confused.

"I'm very sick. I didn't want to tell you because I didn't want it to hinder our flight plans," Binta admitted as she began vomiting.

"How long has this been going on?" Trent asked.

"It started the morning after you took your walk," Binta said.

Remembering what the Lord had told Trent about teaching his children the truth, he knew what was happening.

"Binta, sweety, you're not sick, you're pregnant," Trent smiled.

"Pregnant? No way. Why do you think that?" asked Binta.

"Because I remember when my mom was pregnant with Paisley. She got sick for months. And I do have a sister with children. It makes sense to me. Plus, I think the Lord was telling me something that day I went for a walk," Trent elaborated on his suspicion.

"Do you think I should take this trip?" Binta asked timidly.

"Of course. We'll get extra airsick bags for you," Trent chuckled.

"Do they really have such a thing?" she asked, facing the bucket again.

"Oh yeh, you probably won't be the only one needing those bags," he said as he went over to her and massaged her shoulders.

"I am so embarrassed to meet your family as I get sick," Binta said as she cringed.

"Are you kidding? My family will be excited. They will dote all over you," Trent encouraged Binta.

"Fine. But you better hope I am pregnant and that this isn't some sort of malaria or something," Binta teased as she freshened up and got back into bed.

Two days later, Trent and Binta were seated on the Boeing 747. Pastor Jo had all of the necessary paperwork for Binta in order, and Pastor Rick was waiting in Oregon to help complete the rest.

Once in the air, the two held hands and said a prayer.

"Lord, let this flight be easy on Binta and keep us all safe during these long hours," Trent prayed.

"Amen, Amēni," Binta said in both English and Ethiopian.

CHAPTER TWENTY

Doug pulled his truck to the loading zone at the airport just as Trent and Binta walked out with a cart full of luggage. Abby was grinning from ear to ear and couldn't get out of the truck fast enough. Doug jumped out to start loading their luggage as Abby hugged her son and new daughter-in-law. Doug briefly hugged them as he opened the truck door for them. There were cars lining up behind them, so Doug was trying to rush this process. Once in the car, they were able to talk and formally meet Binta.

"We're going to Trista and Jared's house where everyone is waiting. We figured it would be easier to actually take you to your new home right away," Abby rambled on. Doug softly laughed at his wife's excitement.

"That's great. But what about my belongings at home?" Trent inquired.

"We moved most of your things to your new place. If we've left anything you want, we can always pick it up another day," Doug explained.

"We bought you a brand-new king-size bed, although I'm sure a queen would've been fine. I went shopping with Trista and your grandma, so trust me when I say you have everything," Abby said, smiling.

"What is a king-size bed?" Binta asked Trent.

"It is a huge bed. Nothing like our bed in the hut. It's bigger than the bed we had at the hotel. I promise you'll love it," Trent assured Binta.

Binta noticed the beautiful spring colors and was mesmerized by her surroundings. Trent put his arm around her and pulled her closer to himself.

"We'll actually go for drives so you can see this area up close," Trent promised.

"Binta, have you seen flowers like these before?" Abby asked.

"In pictures only. We didn't get extremely bright, colorful flowers. This is so beautiful," Binta marveled.

They pulled into the long driveway that leads to Trista's house. Trent saw his jeep farthest on the driveway. It made him smile. He was so excited to introduce Binta to everyone that he thought he would cry but didn't.

As they parked, a crowd of people came rushing outside. Binta looked around and was trying to recognize everyone from their photos they had sent to Trent. Binta was a little overwhelmed but thrilled to meet them.

"You're home! This must be Binta," Trista was the first to squeal and hug Binta. "I'm Trista, your sister-in-law."

"Yes, I recognize you from your photos. Thank you for the beautiful clothes. I'm wearing your dress now," Binta said humbly.

"I'm Paisley," Paisley said as she hugged Binta. "I'm your younger sis-in-law."

Binta saw a man hugging Trent and learned it was Neil. Then an older woman walked up and put her arms around Binta, giving her a sincere, welcoming hug.

"I am Trent's grandma and now yours. Welcome to our family Binta. We are so excited to meet you and welcome you. Please, come inside," Jandra led Binta into the house.

Trent walked in and hugged his grandma. He smelled the food and was so excited for Binta to have some real American food.

"You did good, Trent, Binta is a real beauty," Jandra said to Trent as everyone was hugging her and vying for her attention.

"I did, Grandma, and I love her so much. You two have a lot in common. Binta's an artist too," Trent smiled, beaming with pride.

Binta smiled at Trent and, with wide eyes, asked, "Where is the bucket?"

Trent ran to Binta and quickly led her into the nearest bathroom. She used the restroom at the motel the day prior to their flight and in the airport and on the airplane, but nothing was as grand as Trista's guest bathroom.

Trent left after Binta got sick and gave her some privacy. Several moments later, Hanna came rushing into the living room.

"I think Binta's sick. I hear her throwing up," Hanna said in her childlike concern. Her twin, Sarah, was going to check things out when Trista stopped her.

"Trent, is Binta okay?" Trista asked with a strange look on her face. Eyebrows raised and a hint of a smirk. Trista hugged her brother.

Binta walked out and walked up to Trent. She whispered, "I'm sorry."

"No need to be. Everyone, great news! Binta's not really sick, but she is really pregnant," Trent was beaming as he put his arm around Binta.

"What? Congratulations!" everyone whooped and hollered.

Tears were in Jandra's eyes as she hugged Trent. "Meemaw would be so happy," Jandra whispered in Trent's ear.

"I know, Grandma, I know."

Four months later, in August, Neil and Jandra, with Trent and Binta, had their double wedding ceremony. Binta had been seen by a gynecologist who determined she was nearly six months pregnant. She was showing her protruding baby bump, and all thought they needed to have the ceremony before the baby was born. The due date was around Thanksgiving, and they wanted Binta and Trent to have no further distractions.

Neil and Jandra left for their honeymoon the day after the ceremony and would return in mid-October. They had compared their bucket lists and found they both listed the Grand Canyon as number one. That determined where their first stop would be. They wanted to see places like Mount Rushmore, Yellowstone Park, and Glacier Park. They mapped out a way to see them all and have time to stop at any places they may see on their drive. Having the 5th wheel cleaned up and Neil's truck with a fresh tune-up, they were ready to travel. They loaded Winston and Brucy and set off to travel. Trista would take care of Goliath, which Hanna and Sarah were thrilled about.

Abby spent her days with Trent and Binta. She mainly helped Binta set up a nursery. When Binta would nap from exhaustion, Abby would sit in their small living room and talk to Trent.

"Trent, I need to apologize to you for a few things. Mainly about my affair with Rusty. I know his being in our lives was an unnecessary interruption caused by me, but you were the result of that interruption, and I am so blessed by you being my son," Abby said, hoping Trent would understand what she really meant.

"Mom, the Lord showed me that I need to ask *you* to forgive me," Trent began, knowing Abby was trying to ask him for forgiveness.

"Oh Trent, you have nothing to ask me to forgive you for. I need to ask for your forgiveness," Abby said, teary-eyed.

"Mom, I hated visiting Rusty. For years he made fun of God, said racist remarks about anyone he thought was different from him, and in turn, I resented you for making me visit him. I don't resent you now, but I had a seed of hatred growing, and that's what I need you to forgive me for," Trent explained, causing Abby to realize how the depth of her actions affected her son.

"Of course, I forgive you. Please accept my sincerest apology and forgive me as well," Abby half smiled then hugged Trent. They both knew they could keep asking for forgiveness from the other, but that was all summed up when they both understood each other's deep remorse and sincerity. They understood situations in life happen. This one with Rusty was simply an unavoided struggle for Trent. But the struggle was necessary for all involved to draw closer to the Lord.

"Mom, I'm just amazed you got the old guy to repent and receive Christ," Trent said.

"He was ready. Though, sometimes I wonder what would've happened if your dad and I didn't go see Rusty. It was your dad's idea and decision to try and reach him. It was the Lord who primed Rusty's heart to hear what we had to say," Abby stated.

"It makes me realize God does hear and answer our prayers. Sometimes at the final second, but God is never late," Trent smiled.

Trent's cell phone rang, and he answered in a tone that said he didn't recognize the caller.

"Hello?" Trent answered and asked. He listened to the caller ask for him.

"This is Trent McLain," Trent said, then hit the button for the speaker so Abby could hear.

"Mr. McLain, my name is John Nestle, and I am the Probate, or Estate, attorney for Mr. Rus Arnold. The reason I'm calling is that you are listed as the next of kin, and Mr. Arnold listed you as the sole beneficiary of all of his belongings," John Nestle said, introducing himself.

"Beneficiary? Did Rus even have anything?" Trent asked in disbelief.

"Sir, I will have to set up a physical meeting with you to discuss everything. I will need to see proof of identification and have you sign some paperwork. I see you are in Oregon?" John Nestle asked.

"That's correct. Will you come out to me, or do I have to go to Arizona?" Trent blatantly asked.

"I can fly out to you in two days. I just needed to touch base with you and be assured that you are Trent McLain and that I will need to see your Social Security card, driver's license, or some form of identification," the attorney stated.

"Should I meet you somewhere?" Trent asked, trying to be helpful.

"No, I'll come to you," John Nestle said and hung up his end of the phone.

"Mom, that was strange. What should I do?" Trent asked Abby.

"Call Trista and ask for the attorney your grandma met who has helped us. Peter something," Abby answered.

Trent called Trista, and she quickly came over to Trent's cabin home. She understood, and together they called Peter Maxwell, the attorney Jandra had met on a plane trip years ago.

Trista explained everything to Peter, and he said he would take a trip down to Diamond Lake to represent Trent and look over the documents to make sure everything was legal. Two days later, both attorneys sat in Trista's dining room looking over paperwork.

Declaring everything legitimate, Peter Maxwell and John Nestle gave Trent the final results.

"Mr. McLain, by your signing this agreement, you give my law firm permission to sell said properties and to transfer all monies to your personal bank account as the recipient of said items," John Nestle stated, then had Trent sign. Peter Maxwell was also a Notary and stamped everything to become official.

When it was all completed, Peter thanked John Nestle for making the trip, and they exchanged phone numbers and business cards to stay in contact until the estate was finalized.

"We'll give you good news when it's finished, Trent," John Nestle said as he left.

"Trent, Trista, Abby, it was a pleasure to see you all again. I'm sorry Jandra wasn't here. Please give her my congratulations on her nuptials, and I will be in contact as soon as John contacts me that it is over," Peter then said his farewells and left.

Binta, having sat quietly in the adjoining room with Trista's children and Paisley, walked up to Trent and placed her hands on his shoulders.

"So, Peter and John will give you good news soon?" Binta asked.

"Yes, Peter and John will give me good news," Trent replied, then started laughing.

"What's so funny?" Abby asked.

"I never thought I would actually say the words that Peter and John are securing my future. Seems like they did that after they witnessed the resurrection of Jesus Christ and wrote about it over two thousand years ago," Trent laughed, and everyone there heard the irony and laughed with him.

Nearly a week before Thanksgiving, Jandra held a soirée to show everyone photos from her and Neil's travels. She hosted more of a dessert party for the family to spend an evening together. This would enable the ladies to figure out the Thanksgiving menu together. Jandra, realizing she was now the eldest of the McLain clan, said she would prepare the turkey and hold Thanksgiving at her house. The rest was up for grabs. So, Abby, Trista, Paisley, and Binta would volunteer for some part of their upcoming feast.

Binta volunteered to make Mandazi which is an East African doughnut. They're light and airy and taste a lot like coconut. Binta said her mother taught her how to make them, and they were her favorite dessert growing up. Jandra would take Binta grocery shopping to buy all necessary ingredients. She wanted Binta to teach her while she taught Binta a few basic things that Trent enjoyed. One thing they all came to learn is that Binta was a connoisseur of coffee. They learned Ethiopia was known for growing coffee beans. Binta also knew how to make an eggless Tiramisu. But she would start with the Mandazi.

Binta loved spending time with Jandra. She learned so much about Trent's family from her, and Jandra learned much about Binta. Binta was young like Trent, but she had an old soul. She had seen things no one should see, experienced things no young girl should have to experience, and knew hardship and violence like no one Jandra ever knew, including herself. Binta had wisdom beyond her years, unlike any young American girl.

Jandra explained Thanksgiving to Binta, and she enjoyed the history of it. Binta explained to Jandra how she was thankful she survived the Tigrayan Massacre. She asked Jandra to help her understand how she could forgive those that brutally killed her parents, as she felt that her unforgiveness was a hindrance in her walk with the Lord.

"I don't know how to explain that, Binta. All I know is Jesus died to forgive us of our sins, and sin is sin. There's really no said weight of which sin is worse than another. Except to blaspheme the Holy Spirit. But that's very rare to happen with believers of Christ. So, to forgive someone who has hurt us, I can only ask Jesus to forgive them through me. On my own, I can't forgive. With the help of the Holy Spirit and Jesus Himself, I can obediently do it. You will have to seek the Lord and ask Him to help you. My humanity says they don't deserve my forgiveness or yours. But the command of God and His Spirit in mine says I must. You must. Your forgiveness is only for *your* peace of mind to not allow those that hurt you to keep hurting you. Would your mom and dad want you to live with hate in your heart?" Jandra asked.

"No. No, they would not. They taught me to love like Jesus does," Binta said with her eyes slightly glistening with tears.

"Then ask Jesus to help you forgive those that hurt you so they can't hurt you any longer," Jandra said.

"You are a wise woman, Grandma," Binta said humbly.

"I think it's the Holy Spirit using me to speak wisdom to you," Jandra confessed.

Binta hugged Jandra and prayed out loud, "Jesus my Lord, forgive me and forgive in me those that hurt me and my parents. And special thank You for Grandma."

Jandra couldn't stop her tears. Never has she experienced such genuine humility, such sincere prayer. As Jandra held Binta tightly to her, she heard the Lord whisper to her spirit, "Jandra, you just experienced silent, gentle understanding."

Thanksgiving was a pleasant day. The family was all together eating wonderful food. The men were watching football as they snacked until dinner time. For Jandra, it was exceptionally great as she loved seeing Abby and the girls all contribute in some way to make it a special day. Neil was there to carve the turkey and be the man of the house. It all made Jandra have a perpetual smile.

With everything set on the table and the turkey carved, Jandra asked who would like to say the blessing. Binta asked if she could have the honor since this was her first Thanksgiving.

"Dear Lord in heaven, we thank You for this bounty; we praise You for this food and fellowship and ask that You would bless us all with...ah! With the...Ah! Jesus help me!" Binta screamed.

"She's in labor!" Trista yelled.

"Call 911, it's too snowy for us to drive unless we put chains on first," Abby said as calmly as she could.

"Binta, are you okay? Breath like we practiced, honey," Trent instructed.

It seemed to take the ambulance a long time, but they finally arrived.

"Her contractions are about thirty-five seconds apart," Jandra told the EMT lady.

"Okay. Binta, we're strapping you in and will load you into the ambulance. Your husband is coming with us," the nice EMT explained as they were heading out the door.

"We'll meet you at the hospital, son," Doug hollered out to Trent.

Jandra put everything in the oven, microwave, or refrigerator until they could come back home. She was so excited that today was the day the Lord chose to bless her with a new great-grandchild. Jandra grabbed a Tupperware bowl to bring slices of turkey for everyone to snack on in the waiting room. Within half an hour, Jandra and Neil were on their way. Everyone had to either put on snow chains or check the ones they had on their vehicles.

In Neil's truck, Jandra said, "I'm guessing this will be a Thanksgiving Binta never forgets."

"Well, it's true, no matter what it is, you never forget your first," Neil grinned.

In the ambulance, close to the hospital, Binta screamed that she couldn't wait. Within ten seconds and two pushes, Abiona Mary McLain was born. Binta told Trent that Abiona was an Ethiopian name that means *born on a journey*. Truly this was an incredible journey.

CHAPTER TWENTY-ONE

Jandra enjoyed her morning coffee out back, sitting on the bench Neil had built many years ago. She was enjoying the Spring morning, looking at the many flowers that had begun to bloom a month earlier. Jandra often used her morning time to reflect on God's graciousness in her life and the lives of her loved ones. It had been four years since her mother, Mary, had gone home to be with the Lord and three-and-a-half years since a new McLain, Abiona, was brought into the world.

Neil came outside holding a cup of coffee and sat next to his wife. "I knew I'd find you here," Neil said, sipping his coffee.

"I was just reflecting over the past few years and thanking the Lord for His many blessings. I was also admiring the beauty of His flowers," Jandra said and smiled.

"I figured as much, that's why I didn't rush out here," Neil said.

"I also noticed this bench could use a new coat of paint," Jandra smirked.

"I'm way ahead of you on that. I bought a gallon of paint last week," Neil replied.

"Mom used to love sitting out here having her morning tea," Jandra remarked.

"I remember," Neil gently replied.

"Do you know what else I thought of?" Jandra asked.

"I have no idea," he answered with a smile.

"I thought about how far this family has come. Several years ago, there was so much bitterness and unforgiveness. Now, praise the Lord, we are all a loving, happy, content, fully blessed family," Jandra said.

"That's a good way of putting everything. Troubles arise, but this family handles them head-on with God. Even the losses are handled gracefully," Neil added.

"Right. Paisley's birthday is coming up in June. She's going to be sixteen. Do you remember when Trista turned sixteen?" Jandra asked, changing the subject.

"I sure do. That girl wanted to drive and take on the world," Neil laughed.

"I pray that Paisley has similar boldness. Well, maybe not as bold as Trista, but courageous enough to find her way," Jandra exhaled loudly.

"At least Doug and Abby are here to deal with all of what a sixteen-year-old faces. The responsibility won't fall on you," Neil said, kissing Jandra's cheek as he stood up to stretch his legs.

"Hallelujah!" Jandra blurted out louder than she expected to.

"Luya!" the little three-year-old voice of Abiona hollered as she rounded the corner of the yard.

Jandra and Neil laughed as Abiona ran up to them, with Binta following close behind her.

"Good morning," Binta said.

"Good morning. You two are up early," Jandra commented.

"Yes, this little one has been up for a while, so I figured I would take her for a walk to tire her out. Trent left an hour ago for a meeting at church. So Abiona has been running around wide awake," Binta added.

"Do you two want to come inside?" Jandra asked.

"No, thank you, we are going to walk and then hopefully take a morning nap so mommy can clean house, right?" Binta said, looking at her daughter.

Neil and Jandra laughed and watched as the two girls walked away. Neil remembered some morning errands he had to run and asked Jandra if she wanted to join him. Feeling the need to do some house cleaning herself, she declined.

"I'll pick us up some lunch from the deli, so don't worry about making anything," Neil stated, then grabbed his truck keys off of the hook and kissed Jandra goodbye.

Jandra watched Neil's truck pulling away from the house and heading down their long driveway. Smiling, she looked toward heaven and said, "Thank You, Lord, You really have made my life full."

Trent arrived at the church and made small talk with a few of the elders. He was surprised to see them all there. Trent thought this was a meeting for the associate pastors, which he had become last year. Grabbing a doughnut and a cup of coffee, Trent proceeded into the board room, where most meetings were held. Trent noticed an extra empty chair that was placed behind the podium and decided to wait to see who filled it before asking questions. It wasn't long before everyone took their seats, and the meeting began.

"Good morning, everybody. Let's open this meeting with a word of prayer before we begin," Pastor Rick said and then led the ten people present in prayer. After the collective agreements of "Amens," Pastor Rick began the meeting.

"I'm glad you all could make it today. This has been an issue discussed and voted upon unanimously for the past six months.

Trent, I believe you are the only one unaware of this issue, as the issue was actually about you," Pastor Rick grinned as he began, then added, "Actually, the issue *was* you."

"Should I be afraid or honored?" Trent asked half-jokingly.

"I would believe honored," Elder William Stewart said smiling. Elder Stewart was nearly seventy-five years old and has served the Lord most of his life. He was asked to be an Elder ten years after becoming a Deacon in the church, and that was twenty-five years ago. When Pastor Rick joined as the lead pastor in the Klamath Falls church, twenty years prior, they unanimously decided to relocate the church near the Diamond Lake area after they built the new church building. That was nearly ten years ago.

"Why we're here today, Trent, is that we have all noticed and felt moved by the Holy Spirit to anoint you as an Evangelist. We see the call of God on your life and believe you will go far as a witness of our Lord Jesus Christ and bring many souls to believe in Him. We are ready to provide and to send you out as a guest Evangelist to be part of Revival meetings around the world. We have had several churches ask us to be a part of Revivals, but we didn't have an Evangelist to send. We believe we do now," Pastor Rick said, and the Elders agreed.

Trent remembered the Lord had told him on the plane ride to Ethiopia that he was called to be an Evangelist. With tears in his eyes and a grateful heart, Trent accepted the recommendation. Pastor Rick explained that they would hold an ordination service next Sunday at church to introduce Trent to the body of Christ as an Evangelist, and moreover, as the Evangelist for that church, to send out in the name of Jesus.

Trent couldn't wait to tell Binta. He knew their lives were going to change drastically for the Lord. He left the meeting after the Elders had Trent sit in the empty chair while he was anointed with oil. Trent was so filled with the Holy Spirit that he felt a warm wave flow through his body that lasted strongly until he got home. He felt normal as he entered his cabin and saw Binta cleaning in the kitchen. She looked up at Trent and looked at his face and got chills all over her body.

"What happened? I feel the presence of the Holy Spirit on you," Binta said, smiling.

Trent knew Binta was sensitive to the Holy Spirit. Trent told her everything, and together they rejoiced in the Lord. They both sat on their couch as Trent called the family, one by one, to tell them that God was moving and to let them know about the Ordination service to be held on Sunday so they would be prepared and not blindsided. Everyone knew the Lord was doing great things in Trent's life, so they weren't too surprised.

Abby and Doug were talking excitedly amongst themselves when Paisley entered the dining room where they were seated.

"What's going on?" Paisley questioned her parents. They explained Trent's phone call and what the Lord was doing in his life. Paisley listened and took it all in.

"Your brother sure has the hand of God on him," Abby stated.

"Looks that way," Paisley said, now just two months shy of her sixteenth birthday.

"That didn't sound too happy," Abby noted.

"Really? Well, I didn't know what else to say. Trent's always doing God things. It's expected of him," Paisley snapped back.

"Watch the attitude," Doug said.

"Why do you always think I have an attitude? You expect me to clean my room, but you don't get excited about it and call the family when I do it, right? It's expected of me. It's expected that Trent will do great things. Right? So why do you think I have an attitude?" Paisley asked Doug.

"We know that attitude. Remember, your sister and brother were both sixteen. It's a rite of passage," Doug laughed.

"And that's funny to you?" Paisley was really being sarcastic these days.

"I guess not," Doug said and stood up to end that conversation. He and Abby thought about doing some shopping and asked Paisley if she wanted to go with them.

"I have things to do here. Have fun," was all Paisley said as she went back into her bedroom and closed the door.

"I'm glad she's not going. She's becoming a little hard to deal with," Abby admitted.

"She's turning sixteen. I expect nothing less," Doug grinned and shook his head as they both got into their car.

Paisley heard the garage door close, so she came out of her bedroom. Talking out loud to herself, she said, "Good, they're gone."

She grabbed her cell phone and called up one of her neighbor friends, Mandy, to see if she wanted to hang out.

"Hey, Mandy, do you want to come over?" Paisley asked.

"Sure. Are your parents there?" Mandy asked.

"Nope, they went shopping. I figure they'll be gone for a while," Paisley said as she walked into the kitchen and opened the refrigerator.

"Okay, I'm on my way," the girl said as she hung up.

Paisley didn't see anything in the fridge that she wanted to eat, so she looked in the cabinets. She noticed a box of cake mix up on the top shelf, so she got a chair to help her climb up onto the counter. Being able to see the entire top shelf of the cabinet now, she grabbed for the cake box. When she grabbed it, Paisley noticed a small bottle of Irish Whisky cream called Hard Chaw sitting in the corner hidden by stacks of coffee filters and a bag of flour.

Paisley opened the bottle and smelled it. She twitched her nose at the strong smell of alcohol. She didn't know whose it was but figured someone was drinking it. But why hide it? Paisley figured her parents hid it to keep more secrets from her. Paisley was convinced in her mind that her family was always keeping things secret from her. She didn't know why, but she took a big swig that felt like fire going down her chest.

"Gross!" Paisley said, screwing the lid back on, then putting it back in its hiding place. She jumped down from the counter and sat on the chair for a moment. About five minutes later, the doorbell rang, and Mandy walked in through the unlocked door.

"Paisley, I'm here!" the girl yelled out.

"I'm in the kitchen!" Paisley yelled back.

"What's going on?" Mandy asked, seeing Paisley sitting on the kitchen chair.

"I found something," Paisley said, then moved the chair near the cabinets again.

"What are you doing?" Mandy asked as Paisley climbed up and opened the cabinet.

Pulling out the bottle of Irish Cream whiskey, Paisley jumped down and took another swig, then gave it to Mandy.

"Try this," Paisley said, seeming to swig it easier the second time.

"Okay," Mandy took a big swig and handed the bottle back to Paisley after she exhaled deeply.

"I'm not sure what this is used for or why my mom has it, but she's hiding it, and I don't like secrets," Paisley slurred slightly as she took yet another big swig.

The two girls took turns taking drinks from the bottle until there was just a little alcohol left just lining the bottom of the bottle. Unable to stand without swaying a little, Paisley tried to climb back up to put the bottle away. Unable to do it, Paisley opted to hide the bottle in her room then proceeded to get dressed.

"Do you have your car here?" Paisley asked Mandy, who was seventeen.

"Sure do. Do you want to go somewhere?" Mandy asked.

"Oh yeh. I think I need to leave before my barents get pack," Paisley slurred then started giggling.

"I think I'm a little buzzed, so we should go to Zack's house," Mandy stated. She knew Zack as an old schoolmate who was usually home alone because he lived with his older brother, who seemed to never be at home.

Scribbling a note, Paisley said that she was with Mandy. Leaving the note on the kitchen table, Paisley walked out of the front door, locking it behind her.

Mandy began driving down the street in the direction of Zack's house. Zack lived about three miles away, so it was an easy drive, mostly back streets. There was only one main intersection to cross over. Mandy felt her eyelids drooping, and she began swerving.

"Mandy, are you okay?" Paisley slurred.

"Yeh, but I need to call Zack to tell him we're coming," Mandy slurred back and began trying to find Zack's phone number on her cell phone.

"Maybe you shud call 'em when we get there," Paisley slurred, then closed her eyes.

"Okay, but I am thinking maybe I am thinking I was…"
Suddenly a loud crashing sound of metal against metal invaded the atmosphere.

Both girls were knocked unconscious in the car. An onlooker who witnessed the entire crash immediately called 911 to report the accident. More witnesses gathered around to help or to be looky-loos.

One man noticed a cell phone on the floorboard near Mandy. Another was trying to open the car doors but couldn't. There was broken glass and blood on both girls. The driver in the other car didn't have her seatbelt on and was thrown from her car, lying in the street. The ambulance, firetrucks, and police sirens could be heard in the near distance. The crowd backed away as the police got out of their cars, talking to the woman who called 911 and a few witnesses. The firemen immediately started helping the victims. The EMT from the ambulance helped the woman lying in the street. Thankfully, she was alive and only slightly injured with a few scrapes and bruises.

The paramedics couldn't open the doors on Mandy's car, so they broke the back windows to assess the girls. They hollered out to the two girls in the car, but there were no signs of life. Finally, as one paramedic climbed in through the back window, he was able to feel for pulses.

Grabbing Paisley's wrist first to feel for a pulse, Paisley began to move her head and moaned and groaned.

"We have a live one!" the paramedic yelled, and two EMT workers came quickly to assist.

Feeling the wrist, then the neck of Mandy, the paramedic couldn't find a pulse and yelled, "We need a defibrillator on driver!"

Two firemen ran over with crowbars and other tools to enable them to open the driver's door. The same was used on Paisley's door, which opened easier and quicker with the fireman's brawn. EMTs assessed Paisley's condition when they removed her from the car and placed her on a gurney, and saw that she was concussed and had a lot of lacerations and bruises.

They immediately placed Paisley in the ambulance that sped off to the hospital while a second ambulance came for Mandy. The paramedics tended to the lady in the other car and loaded her in the back of the paramedic truck to get her to the hospital to monitor and run tests.

Meanwhile, as the firemen used the defibrillator on Mandy, they couldn't get a pulse. They continued to work on her as they loaded her onto a gurney and put her in the second ambulance. The fireman drove with them as he continued to work on Mandy with the EMT's assistance.

The paramedics, ambulances, and firetrucks all left the scene shortly after, leaving the police to gather necessary information from witnesses and take photos while they called and waited for tow trucks to clear the intersection.

Prior to the arrival at the hospital, one paramedic had found Paisley's purse in the car and brought it with him to the hospital. He also made a note that she smelled of alcohol. The purse was given to the officer on duty at the hospital to locate her identification.

The officer on duty found Paisley's wallet and cell phone in her purse and located the number in her contacts labeled "Mom." He made the call he dreaded to make but was part of his job.

Walking into their house, carrying grocery bags, Abby heard her cell phone ringing. Setting the bag in her arm down, she grabbed her phone.

"Hello?" Abby answered her phone that displayed the call was from an unknown caller.

"Mrs. McLain?" the man's voice said.

"No, this is Mrs. Milner. I used to be McLain," Abby stated, hoping this wasn't a scam call wasting her time.

"This is Officer Dell from the Douglas County Sheriff's Department calling from Mercy Hospital. There's been an accident," the man was saying just as Abby noticed Paisley's note.

"An accident?" Abby asked just as Doug walked in overhearing the word accident.

"Do you have a daughter named Paisley, ma'am?" the officer needed to verify.

"Yes, I do. What happened to Paisley?" Abby started getting frantic. Doug squeezed her shoulder as he bent down, trying to listen.

"She and another young lady were in a car accident, and she has been transported to the Mercy Hospital," he tried to explain, but Abby cut the man off.

"I'm on my way!" Abby yelled and hung up as she and Doug immediately got back in their car and raced to the hospital.

Doug, unaware of the specifics, asked what was going on. Abby tried to tell him but could only scream, "Mercy! Mercy! Mercy!"

The McLain clan all met at the Mercy Hospital waiting room after Doug called for prayer support. It had been two hours since Paisley was admitted, and the doctor told Abby and Doug, they needed to have Paisley admitted for a few days so they could run numerous tests, such as a CT scan, MRI, blood tests, etc. and to observe her. Ultimately, the doctor said Paisley seemed to go in and out of consciousness. The first blood test taken upon admittance showed Paisley had an alcohol level of 0.25 and informed Doug she needed to have her stomach pumped of alcohol so she could vomit instead of losing consciousness. The doctor also informed Doug and Abby that Paisley was way over the legal limit of .08, causing her alcohol poisoning.

The family joined hands and said a prayer for Paisley's safety. Abby, being scared and angry at the same time, was crying and pacing. Jandra walked over to her daughter and put her arm around her, and paced with her.

"I don't get it! Why was she drinking?" Abby asked Jandra.

"Is this the first time?" Jandra asked.

"I think so. I don't even know Paisley anymore, Mom. She doesn't talk to me at all," Abby admitted.

"I have to trust the Lord with Paisley, just as I did with you," Jandra confessed.

"I wasn't that bad, was I?" Abby asked.

"You were worse. My knees are scared up from the prayers I said concerning you over the years," Jandra said.

"Oh, Mom, I'm so sorry. You just don't understand until one of your own kids acts like you," Abby stopped pacing and hugged her mom.

"You didn't act like me, as I didn't drink or use drugs. But my secrets which I kept from you, played a huge role. I didn't realize how much until you began to despise me, and I had to face the truth," Jandra said, then walked toward Neil, leaving Abby to her thoughts.

Face the truth? I guess her secrets were unspoken lies because I didn't know the truth until she revealed it to me, Abby thought to herself.

Abby walked over to Doug in time to see the doctor come out and announce that Paisley was stable and threw up a lot of the alcohol. The CT scan proved she did have a concussion, and they would give Paisley an MRI in the morning. They could visit Paisley in about an hour, two at a time, and not for long. No children at this time.

Doug and Abby were the first to go in when it was time. Jandra and Neil would go next, then Trista and Trent. Binta and Jared opted to stay with the children and asked to give Paisley their love.

While Abby and Doug were in with Paisley, Mandy's parents, Mr. and Mrs. Mandel, entered with the officer on duty who asked for the doctor. When a different doctor came out and spoke to them, Mrs. Mandel began screaming and seemed to be fainting.

Jandra's wave to the officer beckoning him to come to her allowed her to quietly ask what was happening. Knowing they were all part of the same accident, he told her that their daughter was DOA. Jandra silently said a prayer for them.

Abby and Doug came out from Paisley's room, then Jandra and Neil prepared to go in. Jandra noticed that Abby recognized the other woman, and the two of them embraced and sobbed.

Jandra whispered to Neil, "This is just the beginning of the end."

Epilogue

Six months had transpired since that fatal accident. Trent was publicly ordained and sent out by Pastor Rick and the elders. Elder William Stewart passed away one month after Trent's ordination, and Trent was blessed to give his Eulogy. He was also blessed to know that Elder Stewart was given the task of choosing Trent's first tour as guest Evangelist. Elder Stewart chose the England and Scotland's Evangelistic Revival Tour that would last six months. Trent and Binta, along with Abiona, were thrilled to go abroad together as a family to minister.

Binta received her Permanent Residence Card for the United States, which enabled her to get short-term visas for ministerial travels with her husband. She enjoyed being involved in ministry and knew her part as Trent's wife. She was active as a prayer warrior and loved to teach children the truth about Jesus Christ. She had studied at Axum University in Ethiopia for two years to become a teacher but didn't realize her true calling was to be a Sunday school teacher for children to learn about Jesus. Abiona, being three and a half years old when they began going on Revivals, was an attraction for other children when they were in the meetings, and Binta was part of the daycare group provided.

Jared and Trista continued in their ministries. Their three children loved staying with Jandra when she was available. Ethan was a big fan of Winston and Brucy, while the twins, Hanna and Sarah, favored Goliath. They couldn't believe that cat was so huge. They enjoyed trying to put their doll clothes on him. Goliath seemed to enjoy their attention until the dogs would run by barking. Then he was more interested in whatever the dogs were interested in.

Trista and her friend Audrey remained fully active in traveling for the Rape Survivors Seminars. Jared was a great stay-at-home dad, but he often did small handyman jobs at the church. He would join Neil sometimes when Neil would feed the homeless. Jared and Neil became close friends, especially when Trent was traveling. When Trent wasn't traveling, and the weather was warm, the four men of the family would take Neil's boat out to go fishing for a couple of days. Doug was always available to go fishing. Ethan decided that he would wait until he turned twelve to join them. He didn't like fishing, so that was his excuse not to go yet. Jared vowed that Ethan would willfully join them one of those days.

Jandra and Neil continued to attend to their routine hobbies. Neil did a lot of ministry volunteer work and a lot of building things. Mainly whatever Jandra wanted built. His latest was some easels for Jandra and Binta to use to paint larger paintings, along with an expansion in her painting shed to provide a larger working area and to allow more supplies to be stored. Jandra was often commissioned for large paintings for businesses, and Binta was learning to paint portraits. She could draw them life-like, but Jandra was teaching her to paint and mix colors and mediums. Often Binta would carry a sketchbook with graphite and charcoal pencils to sketch whatever fancied her creative mind. Then she'd use her sketches as a reminder of what she wanted to paint. Trent bought her a cell phone to take photos, but Binta rarely used it. God really gave her an artistic, creative gift and a wonderful memory for details.

Jandra and Neil found they were more in love and loved being married rather than just friends. Nothing really changed between them, their everyday lives were the same. But they enjoyed staying warm together in a bed they shared. They both realized their friendship was stronger than ever. They both understood that their relationship was family. Neil and Jandra had enough grandchildren and great-grandchildren to fill any void they could ever think existed.

Jandra often wondered if Neil would miss having a biological child. He would ensure Jandra that he was quite satisfied. Knowing she sometimes felt a little insecure, he took her to a special farm he had heard about that breeds purebred German shepherds. Neil drove with Jandra to Klamath Falls, and he surprised her by telling her he wanted them to have their very own Shepherd puppy together. He knew Winston and Brucy were getting older, so he thought they would pick out a purebred together.

The only stipulation that Neil had was that they get a female and name her Jade. Jandra was thrilled when Neil bought little Jade for her and laughed when he told her Jade would remind them of when they got jaded enough to just get married.

"This is *our* baby, so you can quit pestering me about having one of my own. Capeesh?" Neil asked.

"Capeesh," Jandra said as she held their baby in her lap all of the way home. Little puppy Jade Sheppard, the German shepperd.

Abby and Doug were doing their best to maintain a good, godly attitude after Paisley's accident. For Doug, the challenge was keeping Abby focused on the positive that Paisley survived. But for Abby, there was a hint of survivor's guilt since she was friends with Mandy's mom, Jill Mandel. She was comforting her friend, whose daughter was killed, while in the same accident Abby's daughter lived.

Both women couldn't accept the fact that the girls had been drinking alcohol. Jill figured it was teenage experimentation, and Abby agreed. Abby did wonder if it was Paisley's rebellious attitude as well. Abby refused to entertain the fact that Albert, the abusive drunk, was Paisley's biological father. Abby didn't want to admit there was a chance that Paisley had an alcoholic gene in her body. Abby wasn't even sure if she believed there was such a thing.

Whatever the real reason was, both women agreed to comfort each other and encourage one another to stay positive. After all, they were friends, and they both had other children to think about.

Abby found this to be a great opportunity to witness to Jill about Christ. Jill was an unbeliever, and Abby had a testimony that Jill was fascinated with. Abby didn't share that Doug wasn't any of her children's biological fathers. Instead, Abby focused on sharing that she used drugs and drank when she was younger and how she was very promiscuous years ago. But Jesus Christ saved her from her sins and from being an evil woman. That was her testimony and how she came to Christ. Jill's interest was sparked, but she was still hesitant about accepting Jesus as her personal Lord and Savior. Part of the reason was that Jill's husband was Jewish. Jill didn't know how he would react.

Due to the accident, Paisley suffered a broken ankle that was undetected until she tried to stand on it in the hospital for the first time, as she was trying to get into a wheelchair. Sobered up, she was able to feel the pain and was given X-rays shortly after. The damage was severe and forced her into physical therapy that lasted six months. Paisley had a slight limp on her right ankle that she hoped would dissipate over time. The doctor said if it didn't heal on its own in a few months, Paisley would need surgery to mend the joint and bones. It was her ankle joint that was connected to the three main foot bones that was torn.

Paisley later confessed to Abby and Doug that she and Mandy were drinking alcohol. Since Mandy was older and licensed to drive, Paisley blamed Mandy for bringing the booze. Paisley said that Mandy told her to try it. Once she learned that her friend had died in the accident, she didn't think it mattered who supplied the alcohol. She also figured Mandy couldn't talk, so this was something Paisley swore to herself to take to her grave.

Once she was able to be released from the hospital and had told the police her version of what happened, Paisley had lied so much that she just wanted to be alone. She laid in her bed the evening of Mandy's funeral that she refused to attend by saying she was in too much pain and thought about that tragic day. She knew she had found the alcohol in the kitchen cupboard. Paisley also knew it was her idea that Mandy and she drank it. She also remembered that she hid the bottle somewhere in her room. Since no one said anything to her about it, it must still be there. But where?

Paisley thought about where she may have hidden it. She looked under the bed; it wasn't there. She looked in her clothes hamper; it wasn't there. She looked in her sock drawer, and there it was! Paisley pulled the bottle out and looked at it. She untwisted the cap and smelled it. She didn't know why, but it seemed to call her to swig that last sip. Just as Paisley put the bottle to her lips, Abby opened her bedroom door and walked in.

"Paisley! What do you think you're doing?" Abby screamed at Paisley.

"Uh, I, um," Paisley didn't know what to say.

Abby yanked the bottle out of Paisley's hands and smelled her breath. Abby looked at the bottle wondering why it looked familiar. She didn't say anything as she walked toward the door. Abby was about to exit the room but stopped in her tracks. Turning around with lips pursed, squinting her eyes and pointing her index finger at Paisley, Abby said coldly, "You will *not* be like your father." Then Abby slammed the bedroom door as she walked out.

Paisley sat staring at the door and thought, *What's wrong with Dad?*

More by E. M. Bennet

Secrets Revealed

Every family has secrets. A grandmother, Jandra McClain, who loves Jesus and tries to teach her daughter and grandchildren God's truth, discovers it's her understanding that is in need of a refresher course. Will Jandra trust the Lord enough to reveal her secrets to her family, or will she keep silent to spare herself grief and embarrassment? Can Jandra and her family trust the Lord for healing through it all?

Secrets Revealed is the First Book in the Banquet of Forgiveness Trilogy, about a family that endures real-life issues such as anger, assault, and being judgmental, but most of all, unforgiveness.

Banquet of Forgiveness Trilogy

SECRETS
REVEALED

E.M. BENNETT